ANNETTE

Erskine Caldwell

NEW AMERICAN LIBRARY

TIMES MIRROR
New York

Library of Congress Catalog Card Number: 73-80322

Published by The New American Library, Inc.
1301 Avenue of the Americas, New York, New York 10019

Published simultaneously in Canada by
George McLeod, Ltd., Toronto

Distributed by W. W. Norton & Company, Inc.
55 Fifth Avenue, New York, New York 10003

First Printing 1973

PRINTED IN THE UNITED STATES OF AMERICA

ANNETTE

Part ONE

⤙ 1 ⤚

DURING the recent months of Annette's marriage to Doan Thurmond, while living with him in the large and imposing graystone house on a high terrace in the rolling green hills of Zephyrfield, a quiet residential suburb of costly homes and estates several miles from Doan's law offices in the busy industrial city of Melbourne, there were numerous times when Annette was on the verge of leaving home.

From one day to the next, especially during the past several weeks, it was becoming increasingly difficult for Annette to force herself to keep from going away. She had not said anything to Doan about her distressing unhappiness, but she had seen him watching her questioningly several times recently, and she wondered if he already suspected what was causing her to be so perturbed that she was secretly planning to leave him.

This was not the only period in her life when Annette had had such a compelling and overwhelming desire to run away from home. However, many years had passed since the first time she had seriously considered doing such a thing.

As a very young girl growing up in the small town of Richland, a hundred miles westward from Zephyrfield, Annette had often thought about going away somewhere as far as possible from home and solemnly vowed at the time never to return, no matter what terrible things happened to her or how homesick she might become. There had been many nights when she would stay awake for hours, tossing and turning on her bed, telling herself that she would never be missed because nobody really cared for her.

Even though Annette often had such thoughts, she knew it was not absolutely true that nobody cared for her, because in her heart she never doubted for a single moment that her father really and truly loved her. In the darkness of her room, she wished she could whisper to him and let him know how much she loved him.

The real problem was her mother. In those days it had seemed to Annette that her mother was always trying to invent reasons to find fault with her and thereby have more opportunities to scold her. Even when there was no ready excuse, her mother had often complained that merely being in the same room with Annette was upsetting and made her nervous and brought about all of her headaches.

One particular occasion had been so memorable that during the years following Annette's early childhood there were times when she was unable to keep tears from coming to her eyes whenever something even casually reminded her of what her mother had said in such an angry manner.

This had taken place one evening in midsummer when Annette's mother came to the semidarkness of the front porch and saw her sitting on her father's lap with her arms around his neck and her head on his shoulder. Her father had let her sit on his lap ever since she could remember, but this was the first time her mother had scolded her about it.

But whenever she had seriously considered running away, Annette would become thoughtful and practical and have disturbing doubts about her ability to find food and lodging and clothing away from home.

She had heard talk at school about boys and girls of her age leaving home and being able to live by begging or stealing, but the prospect of having to survive in that way did not appeal to her at all. And even if her doubts had not restrained her, it was exceedingly frightening to hear older girls at school discuss in vivid detail what they had heard about the painful rape and torture and other cruelties inflicted by teen-age boys and brutal men upon girls who were even younger than she was.

The girls at school were inexperienced, but there was an older girl, Susie, who lived in the same neighborhood and knew all about life. When Annette asked her if she thought it would be possible for a girl of twelve to run away from home and be able to take care of herself, she told Annette not to think of doing such a thing until she was old enough to be able to decide what would give her the best chance to find happiness as a female.

Susie had stopped attending high school two years before graduation when she became pregnant and then had a still-born baby. At the age of eighteen, she was a daytime waitress in a small downtown café and a part-time prostitute at night for an elderly taxi driver who solicited business at the highway motels.

"It's true," Susie had said, "that some women get along in life without a man—either because they want it that way or because they can't help themselves. But most women are not like that—we need a man. And that's why there are two kinds of us—loving wives like I'm not, and wide-legged prostitutes like I am. But the main thing is that no matter which one of those two you're going to be, you can't go it alone, without a man. When you get to be like me, you find out that you don't get nowhere in this life and you don't have nothing to live for without a man. It could be different if you didn't have to need a man, but it just ain't that way with me."

After hearing Susie talk about the life of a small-town prostitute as she knew it, and listening to her say how much she regretted not having married, Annette was hoping that very soon she would be in love so she could marry and have children and never be lonely and unhappy and have the regrets of Susie.

All of that, however, was far in the past.

NOW that she was twenty-eight years old, and had twice been married, first to Wayne Lombard and now to Doan Thurmond, Annette was able to convince herself that she could leave home this time and neither Doan nor anybody else would be able to persuade her to go back to live with him in the big graystone house on the high terrace in Zephyrfield.

Annette had already confided in her closest friend, Evelyn Summerall, who was just a year older than Annette and who lived twelve blocks away on the other side of Zephyrfield, that she was uttterly unhappy and wanted to leave Doan after only these few months of marriage and take up her former position as a kindergarten teacher. Doan had firmly insisted before they were married that she would have to stop teaching, saying he wanted his wife to have a normal home life, and reluctantly Annette had resigned in order to please him.

Evelyn, who had been married to Jack Summerall for many years and was busy raising their three children, remained friendly and sympathetic at all times, but she could not understand why Annette would want to give up her marriage so quickly. Moreover, Evelyn had never with a single word encouraged Annette to leave Doan and obtain a divorce.

As Evelyn had said when she talked to Jack about it, Annette had never expressed the slightest hint of dissatisfaction with Doan as a husband. Also, Evelyn had said she had no reason to suspect that Doan Thurmond had ever mistreated Annette in any way or made unreasonable demands upon her or been unfaithful to her since the day of their marriage.

Something else Evelyn had said was that she could not understand why anybody with Annette's pleasing personality and congenial temperament, and who undoubtedly was the most beautiful woman in the whole town, would have the slightest difficulty adjusting to a companionable married life with a handsome young lawyer like Doan Thurmond.

"You go right ahead with your fortune-telling about good marriages and bad marriages by casting horoscopes and such things," Jack had said at that time. "But there's one thing you've got to give me credit for, Evelyn, and that is that I'm too smart to judge a woman's marriage potential until I've had some firsthand sexperience with her."

"You don't have to try to explain yourself to me, Jack Summerall," Evelyn had told him. "I know and you know and the whole town knows that you have to have what you call your sexperiences before you'll trust your judgment."

Even though she was fully aware of Jack's unfailing

interest in personable young women, Evelyn had felt so sorry for Annette after the horoscope had been cast and the future foretold that she did not hesitate to offer to help her in any way she possibly could. It was then that Evelyn assured Annette that she would always be welcome at the Summeralls' if she suddenly left Doan Thurmond and needed a place to stay while making her future plans.

Several times during the past few weeks Annette had actually packed a suitcase in preparation for running away while Doan was at his office in the city.

Each time this happened, at the last moment Annette had turned back before even getting as far as the front door. This was always the time when she felt that she was being pulled apart—half of her body and soul being pulled in one direction and the other half in the opposite direction—and that she could never be her one self again as long as she lived. On her way back to her room, she always had the feeling that half of her belonged to Doan Thurmond and half of her to Wayne Lombard. Then she would whisper, appealing for help.

"Oh, Wayne, I'm so miserable I'd rather be dead. If I have to keep on like this, I don't want to live any longer. I want to do what you said you wanted me to do; but it's Doan—he won't let me. Doan tries so hard to make me happy—but not the way you told me. Oh, Wayne, what can I do—what can I do without you! Help me, Wayne! Oh, please help me!"

Locking herself in her room then, Annette would tearfully unpack the suitcase and put everything back once more in its proper place.

After that, throwing herself face downward on her bed, and pressing her lips into the softness of her pillow, she would stay there sobbing miserably until Doan came home from his office late in the afternoon and pleaded with her to unlock the door.

Even though this behavior had been happening frequently in recent weeks and he had become accustomed to
finding her upset and slightly hysterical, Doan still hoped
that by taking good care of Annette and constantly assuring
her of his love that she would soon recover from whatever
was causing her such unhappiness. In the meantime, he was
never angry and always patient with her while he begged to
be allowed to come into her room and comfort her.

"Annette," he called to her tenderly. "Annette . . . it's
me, Doan. I'm home now, and I want to see you. Please
unlock the door and let me in. Will you do that, Annette?"

Her sobs always became more subdued when she heard
his voice, a signal to Doan that she would soon relent and
let him come into the room.

"Love you, Annette!" he would call to her even more
loudly as he waited at her door in the hallway. "I'm going
to keep on saying it till you believe me."

Then Annette would suddenly become silent, as though
she were holding her breath to be sure she could hear
what he said when he spoke to her again.

"Love you, Annette! Love you!" At this point Doan
was certain that she was listening attentively, and he called
to her so loudly that his deep voice resounded throughout
the house. "Annette! Love you!"

Gradually Annette's sobbing would become so subdued
that soon there was no sound to be heard in her room. This
was when Doan would sit down in a chair in the hallway
and wait for her to unlock the door.

Presently, following a long interval of silence, Doan
would call to her hopefully, "Love me, Annette?"

He would wait patiently before calling again, "Annette!
Love me?"

She had never answered Doan's question, no matter
how often he asked or how long he waited, but he was
always hopeful that she would say something, even though

by that time he no longer expected her to say she loved him.

"That's all right, Annette," he would say to her as calmly as possible, trying to hide his disappointment and hurt. "There'll be time for that later. I'll wait. Just don't forget that I love you, Annette. Nothing can stop that. It'll go on forever. Don't forget, Annette."

There would be another long interval of silence and then, as he expected, the sound of the door being unlocked.

("It's a giant-size wonder that one of several dozen ladies and babes and what-nots in Zephyrfield who're looking for a husband as rich and handsome as Doan Thurmond didn't get to him before that kindergarten teacher came along with the prettiest of everything you've ever seen and fired up his fever. Doan Thurmond could've married a whole dozen of those others if it wasn't against the law to keep that many women in the house—but just look what happened! He picked out that good-looking young schoolteacher and took her home with him like she was Miss American Bedmate herself. Anyhow, he's married to her now, and there's no doubt about it—she's the best-looking girl ever to be seen in this town. What her performance is like in private—well, it could be that Doan Thurmond is the only one who'll ever know about that for sure. But that won't keep me from speculating about it for a long time to come.")

Tall and agile and strikingly brawny, with thick dark hair and a pleasantly congenial smile, all of which gave him an impressive appearance when he went to court as a trial lawyer for a client, Doan was thirty-five years old and exactly to the month seven years older than Annette.

Doan Thurmond had been eminently successful during the ten years he had practiced law, first with a large firm of older attorneys and then for the past few years in partnership with a former law-school classmate, and he was known to be rapidly becoming one of the wealthiest residents of suburban Zephyrfield.

The first time Doan saw Annette was at a party at the Summeralls'. Someone introduced them briefly and then left them, mentioning only that Annette was a kindergarten teacher and Doan was an attorney.

What neither of them knew was that Evelyn Summerall had planned the cocktail party for the express purpose of having them meet. Even the brief introduction had been arranged by Evelyn so that their meeting would appear anything but contrived.

A year had already passed since Wayne Lombard's death. As Annette had confided earlier to Eveyln, she had not forgotten for one moment that he had wanted her to marry again; if possible, within the year, and certainly while she was still young and attractive. Yet here she was already almost past what Wayne had called her "beautiful twenties," with still no prospect of the promised marriage.

At their first meeting at the cocktail party, Annette was aware that Doan was boldly looking her up and down from head to foot and intently inspecting her slender, rounded figure as if making an expert appraisal of her body completely unclothed. She wondered whether she should be angry or embarrassed or flattered by his presumptuous interest in her.

She was still undecided about what she should do when a pleasant trancelike feeling came over her, leaving her no will or desire to demand that he stop. Looking at his thick dark hair and bright blue eyes and tanned cheeks, Annette realized that no matter what his intentions, she herself was completely entranced.

Nervously biting her lips to keep from revealing the wildly intimate thoughts racing through her mind, she knew she was so completely under his spell that if he should ask her what she was thinking, she would blurt out the truth before she could restrain herself.

In the background, the large crowd of guests created a continuous din. When he finally spoke to her, he had to lean so close that she could feel his breath on her ear.

"Your name is Annette? Did I hear correctly?"

"Yes."

Annette nodded briefly as she moved slightly away from him. As she did so, Doan put his hand on her arm as if to let her know that he was going to keep possession of her, and a tingling sensation raced through her body. Closing her eyes momentarily, she wished there would be no end to what she was experiencing for the first time since Wayne's death more than a year before. She had to force herself to keep from boldly grasping his hand and pressing his fingers to her lips, kissing them tenderly one by one as she wanted so much to do.

"Annette!" She looked up at him when she heard him speak her name above the clamor of voices in the room. "I'm glad to know that, Annette. It's exactly what it should be."

"Why . . . why did you say that?" she asked uncertainly.

"Don't you understand? I'm glad that's your name. It's beautiful. It's perfect—the absolutely perfect name for you. Nobody else should ever be permitted to have that name; it should be outlawed for anybody else and belong only to you—to Annette!"

Keeping a firm grip on her arm, Doan watched her closely so she would not be able to make an abrupt move and leave the corner where they stood apart from the other guests.

"Annette," he said, leaning close to her again, "a blessed public-spirited benefactor came along awhile ago and introduced me to you, and I'm going to be forever grateful for that fateful moment in my life. But, be that as it may, I'm not at all pleased and happy with what I heard about you."

"What do you mean?" she asked, astonished.

"You were introduced as being a schoolteacher. But I hope that's not true. Please say it's not!"

"But it *is* true," she said. "Why would you say such a thing as that?"

Doan looked at her with a solemn shaking of his head.

"Then what kind of a teacher are you?" he asked.

"I teach kindergarten," she said proudly.

"Kindergarten! Kindergarten! That's even worse! Little children! I'm very sorry to hear this about you. What a disappointment. And I thought it was going to be my lucky day. But now it's all for nothing."

Annette's large brown eyes sparkled with sudden anger.

"I don't appreciate being spoken to this way. When I was introduced to you, I assumed you were a gentleman, and I certainly didn't expect anything like this. It's most unusual. Why would you say such a thing to me?"

Doan patted her arm calmingly.

"If you'll let me explain . . ."

She tried to pull her arm from his grasp, but he only tightened it.

"Annette, I didn't mean to upset you like this. I should've been more careful about the way I spoke. The trouble is that I've always heard that beautiful young schoolteachers—and especially beautiful young kindergarten teachers—don't stay single for any length of time at all because smart men know they make the best wives to be found anywhere on earth and that's why they're usually already married and—"

"But I'm not married!"

"Thank you, Annette! That's exactly what I was anxious to confirm, and I wanted to hear it said in your own voice with all the emphasis you could give it. Now, I want you to know that I'm better acquainted with you than you think. You see, I came to this cocktail party with the great expectation of meeting you. Otherwise, I—"

"How did you know . . . what did you know about me?"

"First of all, I've seen you downtown a couple of times, and naturally I was curious. Then, as it happened, Evelyn Summerall told me how much she admired you and what a wonderful person you were, and all sorts of other nice things. But one thing Evelyn didn't have to do was describe how beautiful you were, because that I'd already seen for myself. And do you know what I said to myself after seeing you in person downtown and hearing Evelyn talk about you?"

Annette was shaking her head.

"I said that's the girl I'm going to marry," Doan told her. "So now we've met and it's all settled and I'm going to tell everybody that Annette is the girl I'm going to marry."

"I'm not sure I appreciate your—"

"But you are willing to let this cocktail party be the time and place for the announcement of our engagement, aren't you, Annette?"

She was on the verge of saying something, but suddenly turned her head, and putting both hands over her face, began to sob quietly.

"I know tears of joy when I see them, Annette," Doan told her as he pressed his handkerchief to her cheeks. "I can't see any of my own but I can feel some."

She wondered why she was making no effort to push him away when she felt his arm drawing her close to him. An instant later she was glad he was holding her so tightly in his arms, because suddenly she felt faint and weak.

"I think we understand each other now, Annette," she heard him say from far away. "And I have a good feeling that we need each other. I have a liking for you, and you haven't said you dislike me. That's a very promising beginning. Neither of us is married, so let's start from there. I won't be able to thank Evelyn Summerall enough for being right about us."

Annette, with a startled expression, pushed herself free from his embrace and moved backward several steps.

"Why did you say that about Evelyn?" she asked. "I don't understand. What do you mean?"

"My horoscope. She diagramed it for me under the sign of my zodiac. I think that's what she said she did. I don't know anything about the science of it—it's too mysterious for me. But the important thing is that Evelyn was very serious and told me that she had cast your horoscope also and that it was inevitable and inescapable—"

"Do you believe our lives are really ruled by the influence of the planets and the signs of the zodiac?" Annette asked earnestly. "I'm confused about it, but Evelyn is so positive that I don't know what to believe."

"I'll tell you something you can believe in."

"What?"

"First sight. Love at. You know that expression. And you know it so well that you can say it backward like that with your eyes shut, can't you, Annette?"

She found herself nodding dutifully. "Yes, but . . . "

"Don't worry. That's it. First sight. Love at. And after love comes marriage. Just so we're practical enough to go to the proper place and apply for our marriage license."

Doan smiled at her as though absolutely confident of her acceptance.

"You might want to consult Evelyn about the most auspicious date for our wedding," he went on, "but you must keep in mind the urgency of the matter and ask her to arrange it so the planets will cooperate, and set the wedding date right away."

Annette was still too dazed by the unexpected proposal of marriage by a man she had seen for the first time that afternoon to be able to think of anything to say at a moment like that. For one thing, she wondered how sincere such a hasty proposal could be, and finding that Doan had suddenly disappeared, her immediate thought was that the whole thing was a joke. A sudden feeling of despair and loneliness came over her, as if she had been deserted, and her eyes began blinking with tears.

It was only an instant later when Doan was standing in front of her with a glass of champagne and smilingly raising it to her lips. She was so surprised and elated when she saw him that, while she was taking a hurried sip from the glass, much of the champagne spilled over the rim and went trickling down her neck and into the cleavage of her breasts.

While somebody gave her a handkerchief, Doan took the glass and drank the remainder of the champagne with a salute to their future happiness. Soon many of the guests began crowding around them, and somebody poured a glass of champagne on Doan's head. Grinning happily, and reaching for Annette's hand, he made no effort to wipe it from his face.

Evelyn Summerall had come from the other side of the room by that time, and she was busily urging the guests away from the corner where Annette and Doan had been jammed against the wall. As Evelyn left them, she gave Annette a warm smile of approval.

"Annette, this is a very serious situation," Doan said as soon as they were alone again. "Now, tell me which you prefer. Morning or afternoon? It's for you to decide."

"What do you mean?"

"It's lady's choice to say what time of day she wishes to be married. What's it to be, morning or afternoon?"

"I don't know what to make of all this," she said. "You talk as if you take everything for granted. And I'm not even sure I know your name."

"Doan Thurmond."

"Well, it really doesn't interest me to know that now," she told him as she tried to move away. "As I recall, I don't believe we were really properly introduced in the beginning. And it's too late for that. So please excuse me, and I'll be leaving. And I do thank you for the champagne. It was delicious."

Doan reached for her, and Annette resisted for only a moment before letting him hold her so close she could feel the excited rise and fall of his chest and the throbbing hardness of his muscles thrusting against the softness of her body.

"That's a very brave way to talk, Annette, but it doesn't mean a thing to me, and you can't really believe it yourself. And since this has turned out to be our engagement party, let's make it an occasion for getting to know each other. To begin with, I want to kiss you—and that's being intimate. Then I want to take off your shoes and play with your toes—and that's being informal. I consider those two tribal customs worthy of being perpetuated, besides providing a very pleasant method of consummating our engagement.

"Now, to explain more fully what I have in mind, in order to fondle toes properly and obtain the utmost sensual effect for the mutual pleasure of the participating persons, shoes and stockings have to be taken off, which is not the case when merely holding hands. Symbolically, this is an important step, because removing the least item of clothing is historically a socially approved prelude to the practice of love and personal friendship. Don't you agree, Annette?"

Doan picked up several pillows from a sofa and tossed them on the floor behind her. Then, suddenly, without any warning, he had lifted her in his arms, and she found herself sitting on the pile of pillows, her back against the wall. Several glasses of champagne were held one after another so close to her that she was able to sip from one to the next with only a slight movement of her head. As she drank the champagne, the laughter in the room got louder and louder. In the middle distance Evelyn Summerall was floating airily between the floor and the ceiling.

("I've heard that I'm called a meddler and a bleeding heart and a self-appointed do-gooder, and I suppose I am in a way, but ever since Jack and I were married I've wanted to do what I can to help any woman who confides in me when she's terribly upset about something in her private life. Every married woman at some time or other has emotional difficulties, and since that's such a sensitive area, I'm always careful about what I say. I know how desperate a woman can be, and I don't want to be responsible for any woman's infidelity or divorce or suicide. I want to help troubled women, because I've experienced the whole hell of being a victim of infidelity, and it took me to the brink of divorce or suicide.

("What I've said about this explains why I've wanted to help Annette. And helping her does give me a lift and the incentive to keep on hoping for something good to happen to me. This sounds very selfish of me—thinking of myself when Annette was in need of help—but I feel that I'm entitled to blessed happiness as much as any woman. But what I want to say about Annette is that I realized how important it was for her peace of mind to be able to re-marry at a suitable time in order to honor the wishes of her first husband—a death, by the way, which was very tragic—and I felt so sorry for her that I wanted to step in and do something positive about it.

("I had heard some gossip that Doan Thurmond was in the market for a wife to settle down with in that mansion he bought over there on the western slope of Zephyrfield. In my own scheming way, I arranged to be on a downtown street at the same time he was, and a few minutes later we were in a bar having a drink. I don't recall exactly what I said about Annette, but I must have been saying something right, because he became very much interested and asked me dozens of questions about her. In fact, he became so interested that he somehow managed to see her soon after that when she was walking along the street after leaving the school building where she was the kindergarten teacher. Well! The one thing Doan did not ask me was whether Annette was single, married, or widowed, and since evidently his wishful thinking convinced him that she was free to marry, I purposely did not mention the matter. And well! Neither of them was aware of my careful scheming when they were invited to our cocktail party, and I'm sure neither one of them suspected my motives when they met here face-to-face. And you can imagine how pleased I was to see Doan sitting on the floor and playing with Annette's toes half an hour after they had been introduced.")

With her head in a dizzy whirl by then, Annette could vaguely hear Doan saying it had been decided that she was to give notice to the proper authority that she was resigning immediately from her position as a kindergarten teacher. After hearing Doan talk like that she began to wonder how anybody could make such a drastic decision for her without her consent, but time seemed to be passing so swiftly, and she was becoming so drowsy, that she closed her eyes with the contented feeling that she could put off thinking about anything until some other day.

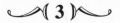

FROM the moment of their marriage, and during all the time they had lived together in the many-roomed high-roofed graystone house on the western slope of Zephyrfield, Annette was positive that Doan was truly in love with her, probably loving her even more deeply than she could realize, and she had no doubt that he would make every effort to please her. Day after day, knowing that he did love her so much, she could not keep from feeling that she was being dishonest and deceitful by not having a similar feeling of love for him.

As evidence of his devotion, for instance, Doan had found out at the beginning of their marriage that Annette was pleased when he brought her flowers when he came home from his office at night. Ever since that beginning, and usually as often as two or three times a week, even when he was busily engaged with an important lawsuit and appearing daily at lengthy court hearings, Doan was in the habit of bringing her a bouquet of red or pink roses.

At the time of their marriage, Annette had explained to Doan that Wayne had wanted her to remarry in the event that he died early in life and that she was doing so for the express purpose of complying with Wayne's wish. At the same time she had told Doan that even though that was reason enough for her to agree to marry him, she had been almost constantly miserable with loneliness during the many

months since Wayne's death and that she dreaded the prospect of having to live alone any longer.

By the time that the several months had passed since
their marriage, and being well aware that she still lacked
any feeling of love for Doan, Annette was distressed to
think how deeply hurt he would be if she left him Whenever she thought about doing such a thing, she would
remember that he had often said he would gladly wait
to the end of time for her to say she loved him.

Annette had become increasingly disturbed and restless in recent weeks, and the time had come when she felt
that she would have to admit to herself that she was
creating, either purposely or unconsciously, her own unhappiness by not being able to accept Doan's love. She
realized what she was doing. She was rejecting him by
locking herself in her room, not because he was Doan, but
because he was not Wayne Lombard.

Finally, as it had come to be in those recent weeks of
distressing uncertainty about her future, even the sight of
Doan, almost as much so as the mere touch of his hand,
was a reminder that she had made up her mind once and
for all time that nobody could ever take Wayne's place in
her heart.

In the past, Annette had never been able to resist him
for the whole night when he pleaded with her and said
he wanted to take her into his arms and comfort her, and it
was a sudden feeling of desperation to escape that had
given her the courage to think she could run away now
before Doan came home and kept her from leaving.

The day had been overcast and gloomy, and as it rapidly
came to an end in the early darkness of the spring evening,
a misty rain was beginning to fall.

Knowing that Doan would be coming home from his
office at any moment, Annette was so fearful that he would

be able to catch her and hold her that she ran out of the house without even taking the time to put some clothing into a suitcase. She did not even want to wait to get her small sedan from the garage.

Carrying only her purse, and running part of the way, Annette had gone as far as the end of the first block on Flower Street before pausing to look backward to see if Doan had already come home, and discovering that she had run away, was following her.

("When I first heard about it, I said to myself that I just couldn't understand how a brilliant young lawyer like Doan Thurmond would let himself be completely overwhelmed by a strange schoolteacher at first sight and be swept into marriage practically overnight. I don't know enough about her to be fair in a critical manner, and so I wouldn't presume to judge her under the circumstances. However, she has no family background in Zephyrfield, and I'm sure she was never invited to any of our social affairs, and none of my friends ever heard of her, until she married Doan Thurmond.

("It has been said, to her credit, though, that she was a widow and not a divorcée—which helps somewhat to give her a slight distinction in these days and times. But aside from that, I must admit that she's a very attractive woman, with youth and personality and an ideal figure to be admired—and envied. I can understand why she would appeal very strongly to a man in a physical way, with her large brown eyes and wealth of long brown hair and her decidedly feminine features. And of course it's no secret to us that a normal man has his own individual method of appraising and testing a woman's sex appeal and potential.

("But what I started out to say was that I was very much surprised that Doan Thurmond—Doan, of all people— chose to marry somebody we never heard of before instead of one of our many lovely local girls. Being acquainted with her so briefly and knowing next to nothing about her mental health, just think of the risk of having her bear his children. The only reason I can think of that would explain why he acted as he did is that he was unprepared to resist all that sexual enticement.")

Still having gone only one block from home, Annette was beginning to realize how thoroughly frightened she was to be alone, while the gloom of the night was steadily coming closer and closer and soon would surround her completely.

"I didn't know it would be like this!" she said to herself in a whisper. "Oh, what's going to happen to me?"

The large houses behind the deep lawns and tall hedges on both sides of Flower Street were dimly lighted through closely drawn curtains and draperies, as though carefully protecting their privacy. Faintly visible, and flickering far away through the leafy branches of the oak trees, only a single street light could be seen.

"Oh, dear God, don't let anything keep me from getting to Evelyn's house! Don't let anything awful happen to me! If I can only get to Evelyn's house, then I'll be all right!"

Annette knew she would have to go almost a dozen blocks along the dark sidewalk in order to reach Evelyn Summerall's house at the other end of Flower Street, which ended at the eastern slope of Zephyrfield, and she blamed herself for not starting much sooner so she could have reached Evelyn's house before dark.

Even though she was becoming increasingly frightened in the night and could not keep from thinking of one horrible thing after another that might happen to her, Annette told herself over and over that she must be brave and keep on going, and not let herself be tempted to run back to the safety of home and Doan's protection.

A sudden gust of wind moaned with a doleful sound in the tall oak trees. It was the wind from the west that came over the rolling hills in summertime and brought a soothing breeze in the heat of the day. In the cold of winter or in the rain of spring, however, the same west wind would sweep over the hills in angry swirls and violent gusts, as if displeased to be forced to come to Zephyrfield in such a dismal season of the year. This time, in addition to its mournful dirge, the west wind was blowing in gusts of stinging wetness.

As she was standing there listening to the relentless sound of the wind and feeling the sting of rain on her face, it seemed to Annette that she heard a familiar voice speaking to her through the wind and rain. She was certain that she could hear the loud pounding of her heart as she looked all around her in fear, and then at the same instant she thought she saw the shadowy figure of a man crouching near a hedge not far from the sidewalk.

Quickly backing away from the street corner and reaching out blindly until she could feel the friendly touch of the oak tree, she waited tensely while wondering if anybody in a nearby house would hear her and be concerned enough to hurry to protect her if she screamed for help.

Annette knew that during the past winter and early spring several teen-age girls and young women had been attacked by a nighttime prowler on the dark streets of Zephyrfield, and there had been deaths by strangulation and stabbing. It was believed by the police investigators that a man was responsible for the brutal attacks, not a woman, but even so there had been no evidence that any of the victims had been raped either before or after being murdered. While the search for the killer continued, girls and women of all ages were constantly being warned of the danger of being alone on the streets of Zephyrfield from dusk to dawn.

Until that very moment, Annette had assumed that such attacks were always made upon other women, and she had never thought that her own life would be in danger. Now she suddenly realized how helpless she would be if she tried to escape or defend herself.

The voice she thought she had heard a few moments before, though, sounded so familiar and friendly that she could not believe that anybody like that would want to harm her.

As she stood there, holding desperately to the oak tree, trying to decide if she should start running or stay where she was and call for help, Annette thought surely she heard somebody speaking to her again out of the darkness in the same familiar voice.

This time the voice seemed certainly to be Doan's, and, relieved from fear but weak from tension, Annette closed her eyes and with both arms hugged the tree and pressed her lips with a grateful kiss to the rough rain-wet bark.

"Annette!"

She was sure once more that she recognized Doan's voice, but she did not want to answer him.

"Annette! Annette!"

After moving a step away from the tree, she looked toward the dim outline of the hedge. This time she was not able to see the shadowy figure she thought she had seen earlier.

"I see you, Annette."

"Go away!"

"Can you see me?"

"No!" she cried out. "I don't want to see you!"

"Love you, Annette."

"No! No!"

"Don't you know who I am?"

"You're Doan."

"And you are Annette. And we belong together. Love you. Don't go away and leave me, Annette."

"I've got to go."

"Why?"

She did not try to answer then.

"I want to know why, Annette," the voice insisted.

"I can't help it—that's why."

"That's not a good enough reason, Annette. Tell me exactly why you are running away."

"You are not Wayne, and so——"

"Of course I'm not Wayne Lombard!" The sound was provoked and angry. "I don't even look like your pictures of him that you're always showing off, for Christ's sake! But if that's what you thought, why in hell did you marry me? Why did you let me think you'd love me? How did you ever get the idea in your head that you could make me a substitute for a dead man?"

"I married you because Wayne wanted me to. I mean, Wayne said he wanted me to marry somebody after a year if he——"

"That's plenty goddamn silly. What the hell! The guy is dead and gone. How could he have anything to do with it after he's been dead a year? It's foolish to ruin your life by making a martyr of yourself because of a bygone love affair that ended a long time ago in death."

"You don't know how much we loved each other for such a long time. And that's why I don't want to fail now to do what Wayne wanted me to do."

"You married again. That takes care of it."

"But that's only part of it. Wayne wanted me to have three children, but you won't let me have even one baby."

"And you know why, too. I've told you. I'm not convinced that it would be wise. You're always saying you can hear sounds and conversations that nobody else can hear. And you're whispering out loud and talking to yourself half the time. Well, I don't know how much of this was passed down to you by your mother and how much of the same would be transmitted to a child of mine if you were the mother. Hereditary traits——"

"That's insulting! I won't listen to any more of that. Leave me alone and let me go."

"Where are you going?"

"I won't tell you. I don't want you to follow me."

"I'm not sure you know what you're doing."

"Well, I know."

"And I know it's dangerous for you to be out on the street alone at night, Annette. I don't want anything to happen to you—I love you so much."

"You can't scare me and make me change my mind."

"Then will you tell me just one thing, Annette?"

"What do you want to know?"

"Are you going to Evelyn Summerall's house?"

"Yes."

"That's where we met the first time."

"Of course."

"I'm going to be waiting and hoping it'll be like that again. Champagne and your toes to fondle and all that. Do you hear me, Annette?"

"I can hear you very clearly, Doan, but I can't see you. Where are you?"

"Wherever you want me, I'll be waiting for you and hoping. Isn't that enough?"

Part TWO

✦(1)✦

IN the beginning, Wayne Lombard and Annette had been so youthful and so much in love that it had never occurred to either of them to wonder why they had suddenly become so passionately attracted to each other almost at the same moment. Nor would they have wanted to be reminded of their previous attitude of mutual indifference.

All of that had taken place in the past; the only thing of importance now was to experience the happiness of being together.

As if by accident, and with no forewarning at all, Wayne and Annette had first of all been amazed and then entranced when they discovered together that the slightest touch of their hands mysteriously produced a strange and exciting sensation that raced through their bodies and minds.

It was soon after discovering that such bliss and pleasure could be produced by the merest touch of their hands that they tried for the first time to express their love for each other. Words came slowly and painfully in the beginning, and it was much easier for both of them to let a glance and a touch speak for them when words failed.

("It gives me a feeling that I'm peeping and spying and doing something I shouldn't when I watch Annette and

that Lombard boy walking by. Every time they go past my
house, I always wonder what they talk about when an
older person like me can't hear them. They don't seem
to be ever saying much, though, and maybe just being
together is more important than a lot of talk. I must be
purely romantic, because I get a spell of trembling when
I see a young girl and boy like them shyly holding hands
and trying not to be embarrassed when people stop and
stare at them. Whenever I see that happen, it makes me
remember when I was young like that, although in those
days we didn't dare hold hands in public where we'd be
seen and talked about.

("There's something else I often think about when I
see Annette coming home or leaving to go somewhere. I've
observed her ever since she was a small child, and every
year she gets to be more beautiful. At this stage in her
life, she's already an outstanding beauty, and goodness
knows what she'll be like a few years from now. Well,
that's one thing to think about, but there's something else
about Annette that's so very strange. More and more, I've
seen her leave the house across the street and come out
to the sidewalk and stand there for a long time talking to
herself. I can't hear what she's saying, but I see her lips
moving, and she gestures with her hands, and I'm positive
she's saying something out loud.

("I consider that a strange thing for anybody to do, but
it happens so frequently that I can't keep from wondering
what connection there might be between Annette's strange
behavior and her mother's condition. As everybody in this
part of town knows, her mother's condition is not at all
good, and she's had quite a few disturbed spells and takes
treatment for them whenever they occur. And since undoubtedly Annette is going to be an unusually beautiful
young woman, I hope she can avoid anything resembling
her mother's condition.")

Annette and Wayne had soon come to find out that

words, in addition to the touching of the body, were also important, and this was when they had solemnly vowed to be faithful sweethearts as long as they lived.

As deeply earnest as they had been at the time, and as serious as they had considered the circumstances to be, they had often joked in later years about their youthful concept of how to go about making an everlasting vow and memorializing it without a traditional engagement ring. The vow had been made by sharing a double-dip chocolate-chip ice-cream cone.

For more than a year before that memorable spring when Wayne Lombard came into her life, Annette had been restless and morosely unhappy. And as a result of her frequent spells of discontent that always followed her mother's criticism of her, there had been many times during that past year when she came very close to running away.

Fortunately for her, at such an early age, what would cause Annette to change her mind when she was on the verge of leaving home would be something frightening overheard at school—stories relayed in whispers from one girl to another during recess or repeated on the way home from school. The tales would be so grossly horrible in the telling that they would make some of the girls have scream- ing nightmares.

What had frightened Annette so much at that particular time in her life and had made her afraid to leave home was hearing a girl of her own age describe in vivid detail what had happened to one of her friends who lived in a nearby town. The girl had dropped out of school at the age of fifteen and started out one morning to try to hitchhike to a commune she had heard about in a city hundreds of miles away. What was so horrifying to Annette was hearing about the girl's mutilated body being found only a few miles from home in a field where she had been tied with a rope and raped and stabbed to death.

All this had taken place in a difficult period in Annette's life when frequently she would say she was ill or make some other excuse in order to avoid helping her mother with the household chores. Her mother was a thin, quick-tempered woman in her early forties then, nearly always carelessly dressed and indifferent about the care and appearance of her short yellowish hair.

At those times when her mother became provoked and threw pots or dishes at her, Annette would go to her room and lock the door and stay there until her father came home to do all he could as a peacemaker. After listening to everything Annette and her mother wanted to tell him, he had remarked several times in a joking manner that it was a pity he and her mother did not have other children to take her place so they could be unselfish and approve of her going away to find a better home for herself somewhere else in the world.

There were times when Annette and her father were alone in the house, and then she would come close to him and look at him with tears in her eyes. Such intimate moments occurred only when her mother was sent to a rest home by their family doctor for a week or longer in the hope that it would help her calm her nerves and regain her health.

"Daddy, if anything ever happens to Mama," Annette had said pleadingly several times while her mother was away, "please promise me you won't marry anybody else like her. I just couldn't stand it if you did. I'd do something—I don't know what! I hate Mama so much, and I just wouldn't want to live if you married somebody else exactly like her. Will you promise me that, Daddy?"

He stroked her long brown hair soothingly for a while before speaking to her.

"You shouldn't feel like this about your mother, Annette," he told her kindly after that. "She doesn't hate you. She really loves you. And you shouldn't hate her. If she's disagreeable sometimes, just remember that she doesn't always feel well. That's why it's best for her to spend as much time as possible at the rest home. As people grow older, they can become easily upset when their health bothers them. Remember that, Annette. And try to get along with your mother, no matter how much she fusses at you. Try to be kind to her."

"I don't want to be kind to her."

"Nobody can make you be kind to her, Annette, but the least you can do is have a little sympathy for her—in her condition. After all, she's been taking care of you ever since you were born."

"I'd rather have you take care of me, Daddy. I love you, and I can't help it if I hate her so much."

"I love you, too," her father told her, stroking her flowing brown hair over and over. "You are my precious little girl and always will be—Annette, my Annette! I'll do everything I can for you while you're growing up, and then I'll miss you very much when you fall in love and marry and go away. And no matter how much I'll miss you, I will be glad when I know you're happily married to somebody who loves you and appreciates you."

"Daddy," she said, cuddling close to him, "Daddy, I think somebody already really loves me like that. Wayne and I . . . It makes me feel so excited when I think about it. . . ."

Annette suddenly reached for her father's hand and was kissing each of his fingers time after time.

"Are you glad now that you didn't run away from home?" he said rather gruffly, making a pretense of scolding her for even thinking about doing such a thing. "Aren't you glad you're still here?"

"Yes, Daddy!"

"Well, I don't want to try to make you promise anything," he had told her then in a serious tone of voice, "but I hope you'll stay right here till you graduate from high school, and after that, go off to college. And then, somewhere along the way, you'll surely decide you want to marry—when you're old enough for that, of course."

"Daddy, you're so wonderful to me—you talk like you really and truly love me. I can't marry you, and that makes me so sad. And so what I want is for Wayne to be just like you. I couldn't feel the slightest love for anybody who wasn't exactly like you and Wayne."

Now that she was so much in love, tears had been quick to come to her eyes and trickle down her cheeks when she was reminded what might have happened and how much she would regret it then if she had let herself run away from home. Tense and concerned, she could not keep from thinking how tragic her whole future life would be without Wayne Lombard and his love for her.

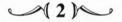

ANNETTE, slender and graceful, and with a feminine beauty that was vivid and appealing, was only fourteen years old when she first met Wayne Lombard. Already tall and muscular, with blond hair and blue eyes, he had recently reached his sixteenth birthday and would soon graduate from high school.

Wayne's family and Annette's parents lived only a few blocks apart on the same narrow, treeless street in similar one-floor white frame houses on the west side of Richland, a town of several thousand persons surrounded by chicken farmers and dairy plants and cheese factories. Annette and

Wayne Lombard had always attended the same school in Richland, beginning with the first of the elementary grades, and yet they had not even known each other's name in those early years.

Their parents were in the habit of nodding in a friendly fashion or speaking casually to each other on the street, but there had never been contacts of a social nature between them.

Annette's father had been a journeyman carpenter early in life and later became a local building contractor with limited success. Wayne Lombard's parents, who were raising a family of several children, owned and operated a small merchandise and variety store on the principal business street of Richland.

Having promised her father to stay at home until she had graduated from high school, and still only fourteen years old at the time, Annette had wanted to earn as much money as she could in order to help her father pay for her college education, and she began ironing and mending clothing for some of the neighbors. What she liked to do best of all, and whenever possible, was work as a mother's helper in homes with several small children.

As for Wayne Lombard, he was working, just as Annette was, to earn enough money to go away to college after graduation from high school. When not attending classes, he worked at his parents' store unpacking crockery and hardware and variety goods, and once a week it was his job to select and install merchandise for the window displays.

It had been midsummer when Annette and Wayne began saving the money they could earn toward college expenses. By that time they had been seeing each other almost every day for several months, and they were sure ways could be found so they could be together every possible moment in the future.

When there were times they could not be with each other

that summer, Annette on several occasions had gone to her room and locked the door to prevent her mother from being able to walk in and find out what she was doing. What Annette liked to do in the privacy of her room was pose in front of the large mirror on the wall and view herself as she repeated in a guarded whisper everything she could remember that she and Wayne had said to each other the last time they were together.

Sometimes sitting in a chair fully dressed, and at other times completely naked, and often for as long as an hour, she could recall vividly almost everything they had said and done together ever since that memorable first time when they walked home from school.

("It's bad for my nerves not to know what in the world Annette does when she goes in her bedroom and locks the door for an hour or more. All I know about it is that she won't open the door when I try to go in there so I can find out what she's making such a mysterious secret of. I've thought of a lot of reasons why she'd be making such a big secret of what she's doing in there. She could be writing love letters to that Lombard boy, or playing with her own sex, or practicing some way to wear her clothes, or pretending to be doing something that I don't know anything about.

("Some of the time I'm positive I can hear faint whispers that can only mean that she's talking to herself. Anyhow, I always get a terrible headache trying to listen and find out what she's doing in there. I get so upset and nervous that I feel like screaming at her and doing something to make her let me in that room to see for myself. When she's not in her room and I say something to her about it, she shuts up real tight and won't say a word and acts like it's none of my business what she does in her room with the door locked.

("This behavior of hers has been going on almost since the day the school was out for the summer, and that was the beginning of when that Lombard boy started hanging around her, and that makes me think the way she's behaving has something to do with him. I've got my notions about what they could be getting ready to do about sexing. Now, what I want done is to get that lock off her door so I can get in her room in a hurry if that Lombard boy hangs around her too much to suit me and I see signs that make me suspicious that sexing between them might get started.")

So many times had Annette gone to her room and locked the door that summer that her recollection of the time when she and Wayne discovered each other seemed to her to have become as real as it had been when it actually happened.

Facing the large mirror on the wall and speaking in a whisper that she hoped could not be heard beyond her own room, Annette would excitedly describe in minute detail what had taken place that sunny afternoon in late spring a short time before the end of the school term and the beginning of summer vacation. She was able to recall every sight and sound so clearly that she knew she would never forget the first time she and Wayne Lombard had walked home from school together.

Usually at that moment, and before she could go any further with what would start out as a perfect rehearsal, there was always a lengthy pause when she had to suppress a sob before being able to continue. What always brought tears to her eyes was the unpleasant reminder that before the first time they walked home together they had always studiously ignored each other as if neither of them existed.

What was so distressing to Annette was the unpleasant recollection of the time she and Wayne had wasted by not being together and getting to know each other sooner. As sad as she was for the wasted opportunity, she always felt very happy when she could finally wipe away her tears and smile as she began thinking about the day when she and Wayne were together for the first time.

Their meeting had taken place as they were leaving school in the late afternoon and were walking toward home on the same side of the street. It was an awkward moment, embarrassing to both of them.

After going several blocks in silence, Wayne stopped, shortly before reaching Annette's house, and looked at her wonderingly for several moments, as if unable to decide if she might laugh at him if he told her what he wanted to say. Annette glanced at him shyly several times, smiling helpfully, but still without the courage to be the first to speak.

Finally, Wayne cleared his throat with a nervous cough.

"I guess I look . . . I mean, I guess I look like I'm being sort of silly . . . or something like that. I'm not used to doing this. . . ."

Annette felt almost compelled to reach out and touch him with her hand. She did move closer to Wayne, but all she was bold enough to do then was to look up at him admiringly with an encouraging smile.

"It's all right to talk about anything you want to," she said. "It's what I want you to do. Just go ahead and say it—say anything."

"Well, I know who you are," he had said, as though he had made a valuable and unexpected discovery. "Your name is Annette."

She nodded eagerly, continuing to smile at him.

"And there's something else . . ." he said hesitantly. "It's another thing . . ."

"What is it?"

"You're pretty—real pretty!"

Annette, bowing her head instantly, covered her face with both hands.

"Wasn't it all right to say that?" he asked quickly.

Lifting her head and looking up at him with her big brown eyes, she was again smiling eagerly.

"Of course," she told him. "But I didn't know you'd be saying anything like that."

"Well, I wanted to say it, because that's what I think." The worried expression on his face was rapidly disappearing. "My name is Wayne. Wayne Lombard."

"I know that."

"You do?"

"Yes."

"Well, I guess that's the way it ought to be. I knew your name, and you knew my name. And another thing is that I've seen you a lot of times before."

"Me, too." Annette was quick to laugh at herself as soon as she had spoken. "But not that! I don't mean I've seen myself—I mean I've seen you many times. That's what I really meant."

"Well, anyhow, I'm sort of glad the way it is now," Wayne said with a lingering stare.

"Why?" she asked, glancing up at him as she moved slightly closer to him. "Why are you glad . . . Wayne?"

He smiled instantly with a pleased blinking of his eyes as he heard her speak his name. A moment later he had moved closer to her.

"Wayne, please tell me why you're so glad," she urged.

"Well, it feels real good to be going along the street like this with you now. I didn't know about it before. It sure is nice like this. Sort of the way you feel when you're doing something you like doing a lot . . . what I mean is, like doing something you'd rather do than have to do something different. I don't know how else to say it exactly. But that's the way I feel, anyhow. Maybe you know what I'm talking about."

"Of course, Wayne. I know. And I like being with you, too. Maybe we feel the same way about that. And maybe that's why I'm so sure I know what you mean. And maybe there are a lot of things we feel the same way about—all kind of different things. It'd be real nice for us to be like that—the same way. . . ."

He turned to her with a lingering, grateful gaze.

"Annette, if it's all right with you . . . I mean, if you want to . . . I'd like it to be just like this again. And real soon, too, exactly like it is now."

She was too excited to say anything then. They walked the several blocks to Annette's house in silence. Just as they reached the house and Annette was leaving Wayne at the sidewalk, their hands touched briefly for the first time.

Almost immediately after that startling experience, Annette left Wayne standing on the sidewalk, and without a single word or a backward glance, ran excitedly into the house.

The following afternoon they again walked home from school together, and the day after, and then every day of classes until the end of the school term. In the beginning they had gradually begun shyly letting their fingers brush together, and soon they were boldly holding hands as they went down the street.

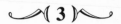

(3)

NOT long after their first meeting, late one afternoon Annette and Wayne were standing at the doorway of her house. Suddenly locking his arms around her and holding her so tightly that she could barely breathe, Wayne kissed her. For a long time Annette had been waiting patiently for his kiss. Now she gave herself eagerly to his embrace. Still almost breathless with excitement, she kept her eyes closed while first he kissed her mouth and then her cheeks and neck and again the fullness of her warm lips. All at once she wanted to tear away the clothing between them as she felt the stroking of her breasts and the thrusting of muscular hardness into the yielding softness of her body.

Neither of them was completely surprised at what had happened. Annette had been hoping from one day to the next that Wayne would hurry and kiss her and hold her in his arms for the first time. She had often tried to imagine what it would be like when she felt the closeness of his body. Now, while trying to think only about how happy she was being with Wayne and wanting to keep all distracting thoughts out of her mind, she could not keep from wondering if what was taking place was real or whether she was dreaming.

Even when she opened her eyes and could see Wayne and assure herself that he was actually holding her in his arms, Annette still was afraid that she might wake up and find that she had been foolishly recalling something that she had merely imagined and was trying to make herself believe was true.

Both of them were tense and trembling slightly when Wayne finally relaxed his embrace. As if the withdrawal of his arms had stricken her painfully, Annette immediately put her arms around his neck, pressing her body as close to him as she could, and clung to him with a desperate cry.

"Wayne. Oh, Wayne . . ."

"What is it, Annette?" he asked.

"Tell me, Wayne," she whispered. "Tell me it's real."

"You mean being here like this?"

"Yes!"

"It's real. Of course. Why did you say that?"

"Wayne . . . you won't think I'm foolish, will you?"

"Well, I haven't thought so yet. Why?"

She tightened her arms around his neck and drew the hardness of his body closer to her.

"I've been imagining so much about us, Wayne. It seems like I've been imagining every possible thing in the world about you and me and us together. And when I think about certain things, I don't always know if they've really happened or if I only think they have—like in a dream. That's why I get so mixed up. I like to think about us, and then, when I get started doing that, I don't want to stop, and so I keep on and on and on so much that I have to believe what I was thinking. But you really and truly don't think I'm foolish, do you, Wayne?"

"I don't know how foolish you are—maybe just a little bit—but you've got a strange way of talking about us. I mean, when you say you've been imagining or dreaming or thinking about certain things. But maybe you can make the things you want happen that way. Anyhow, you're so beautiful and so nice to look at and be with that I think about you a lot, too."

"Are you sure you think nice things about me, Wayne?"

"You bet I do. You're the nicest thing of all to think nice things about."

With a shiver of joy, Annette pressed her face against his chest.

"Do you love me, Wayne?" she whispered quietly with a cautious inflection of her voice that sounded both wishful and apprehensive of what his answer might be.

"Well, I feel like I do."

It was several moments before she could begin breathing normally again.

"Why do you love me, Wayne?" she asked then.

"I don't know . . . exactly. It's just the way it is."

She pressed her body closer to him.

"You haven't really told me that . . . you haven't really said it yet."

"Well, if that's what you want to hear, now's the time to listen. I love you, Annette, I love you."

As she raised her head from his chest and looked up at him, Wayne kissed her eagerly. After that, she looked at him lovingly with a blinking of her large brown eyes.

"I want to tell you something, Wayne," she said.

"And I want to hear it. What is it?"

"It feels so good to be like this with you."

"I'll say the same thing."

"And I mean it with all my heart, Wayne."

"Me too."

"Will you always?"

"Always."

Nothing more was said after that for some time. Then Wayne gave her a tender pat on the cheek.

"Annette, tell me something. Tell me it's all right for me to want you like I do . . . the way I do."

"It's all right for you to want me the way you do."

"Why is it all right?"

"Because I want you the same way, Wayne."

"How do you know what I mean?"

"All I know is that I want you to wrap me up in a bundle and take me somewhere and put yourself in me where you belong and let me hold you in my arms while you're doing that so I can keep you close to me like a little baby and then I can love you so much I'll be happy the rest of my life."

Wayne leaned over her and kissed the top of her head. Slowly and lovingly he stroked her flowing brown hair. Annette could feel the aroused throbbing of his body against her thighs. She began eagerly kissing, one after the other, all the buttons of his shirt that she could reach with her lips.

Presently, after unbuttoning the whole length of his shirt, Annette pressed her face contentedly against his chest, as

Wayne gently stroked and squeezed the flesh of her thighs with both hands. Still no word was spoken by either of them. Finally Wayne took her arms from his neck and lovingly patted her flushed cheeks.

She waited until he had stepped backward and was standing several steps away before she spoke to him.

"Wayne . . ." she began with a hesitant smile, "Wayne, do you think I'm beautiful?"

"I've heard that all girls are beautiful at certain times, certain places, and things like that."

"But what about me right now?"

"You are very beautiful."

"What else?"

"You'll always be beautiful to me."

"And then what else?"

"I want every inch of you."

"What would you do with every inch of me?"

"What would I do?" he said with a quick smile. "Well, first of all, I'd do the natural thing."

"What is the natural thing, Wayne?"

"Kissing you good . . . to start with. . . ."

"Don't wait, Wayne," she said in an eager whisper as she looked up at him. "Do it now. Kiss me good."

A trembling smile came to her face as she first felt the tingling touch of his hands moving caressingly over her body, and she was quick to help him put his hands under her dress so both of them could feel him stroking the bareness of her legs and breasts.

"Wayne, don't stop," she pleaded. "Don't stop what you're doing—do everything. I want to feel you doing that all over me—every inch of me, like you said you wanted to do. That's what I want, too. I'll do anything for you—everything. I want to kiss you all over—everything of you, Wayne. I mean it. Please let me do it the way I want to—where I want to—everything . . . that's what I want most of all right now."

Several loud blasts of an automobile horn broke the late-afternoon silence, as somebody drove slowly down the street. Startled by the sound, and realizing that they had been standing on the porch in full view of anybody passing the house, Wayne hastily moved aside, wondering if he and Annette had been seen while they were being so intimate.

"I guess I'd better be leaving now," he said nervously.

"But you don't have to go," Annette told him, putting her hand on his arm. "I wish you'd stay a little longer, Wayne."

"Well, I don't want to go," he said slowly. "But I'm afraid of . . ."

"Of what?" Annette asked.

"Going crazy about you like I am."

"Then stay here and go crazy about me—don't go off and do it where I can't see you. I don't want you to go away and leave me. I'd be so lonely without you now. You'll stay, won't you, Wayne?"

"I don't want to leave yet. But we can't stay here like this. It's not private enough out here on the front porch. Somebody might see us and tell about it."

"We can go inside," she said at once. "Then we'll be out of sight, and nobody can see us and say anything about us."

"I don't want to get caught in there. Your folks . . ."

"It's all right, Wayne. Don't be scared. Mama's not here now. She's visiting somebody on the other side of town, and she won't be back for a long time. Don't worry about her."

"But what about your dad?" he asked then.

"Daddy never comes home this early. Don't be afraid, Wayne. It's all right. Let's go inside.

"Well, if you think it's all right," he said uneasily. Then his voice brightened. "One good thing about you is that you don't have a bunch of sneaky brothers and sisters to come snooping around where they've got no business."

"I don't need any brothers and sisters," Annette said, smiling. "Because all I need is you—and now I'll never need anybody else in the whole world as long as I live."

Wayne frowned and shook his head.

"What's wrong?" she begged instantly.

"I was going to say that—exactly like that—about not needing anybody else."

"You can still say it, Wayne."

"No," he stated emphatically. "You said it first and better and quicker."

"Wayne! You're so wonderful!" She was looking up at him with delight. "You're my dearest, dearest, dearest sweetheart!"

"What other kind have you got?" he demanded with a sudden glumness. "I didn't know there was more than one kind. And if I'm not the only one . . ."

"No! Not that!" She looked at him appealingly. "Wayne! I didn't mean to say the wrong thing. It's not like that at all. Please believe me."

"I don't know if you're telling the honest-to-God truth or not. How would I know how many boyfriends you've got around town? But if you think you can keep a whole bunch of them hanging around you . . ."

"Please believe me, Wayne. I didn't mean it to sound like that—not like you think—not a word of it. You're so dear to me—that's why I wanted to call you that. There's nobody else—only you. Now you believe me, don't you, Wayne? Please say you do!"

"Well," he said presently, speaking slowly and not looking directly at her, "well, if you say you really mean that, and if that's the honest truth, I guess I'll believe you this time. But it had better be the truth, because if I ever find out something different—and if you ever let anybody else get to you—and you know what I mean . . ."

"No, Wayne, never," she told him with a sob in her

voice. Her large brown eyes were blinking rapidly, and already there were teardrops on her cheeks. "You mustn't think anything like that about me. You must believe me, Wayne. You've got to. I'll say it a thousand times if you want me to—there's nobody else. That means only you—and us. Now, come on with me, and let's go inside. It'll be all right in there. Don't worry about it." She reached for his hand and drew him toward the doorway. "Come on with me, Wayne."

STILL holding his hand, Annette took Wayne into the hall and led him directly to the door of her bedroom. The curtains over the windows were almost completely closed, and there was so little of the late-afternoon light visible by that time that the room at first appeared to be in total darkness.

Wayne's eyes were gradually becoming accustomed to the dim light, and after a while he was able to see the outline of Annette's wide bed near the center of the room.

In addition to the queen-size bed, there were several chairs in the room, and on a bedside table a tall reading lamp with a bright pink shade. The largest chair in the room was placed in front of a dressing table, and on the wall above the table was a gilt-framed mirror so large that it reached almost to the ceiling.

Annette closed the door and drew him toward the bed.

Wayne saw for the first time that the wide bed was

covered with a pink spread almost the same color as the
lamp. Propped up against the headboard, surrounded by
several plump pillows of various shapes and shades of pink,
was a huge black teddy bear with large gold-colored ears
and shining green eyes and a grinning expression on its
face.

Even propped on the bed with its legs stretched out in
front, the bear appeared to be almost the same height as
Annette, though much more chubby in girth, and its grinning expression was so lifelike that Wayne could not keep
from staring at it in wonder.

("Almost every week for the past several months I'd
look out my window and see Annette coming and going
on the other side of the street. And whenever I watched
her go into her house or leave it, that's when I'd say to myself that it was going to be only a matter of time till
Annette attracted a wide-eyed boy with that oh-so-sexy
bounce of her girlish little bosom and perky behind. And
at barely fourteen, too! Some people will say a girl like her
has no control over her early physical development and
that otherwise she's normal for her age and should continue to be treated like a little girl. In theory, maybe so.

("But there's more to it than that. I've heard she keeps
a big life-size teddy bear in her bed and sleeps with it every
night and even puts pajamas on it just like it was human.
You'd think nothing of it if she was a little girl of five or
six, or even as much as ten years old, but she's a big girl
now. And if you ask me, I'd say that enormous teddy bear
is a substitute till some boy comes along with the real thing
she's after. Just imagine, pajamas and all. Annette's a very
strange girl, and no wonder—just look at her mother!")

Wayne was still looking at the grinning black bear when
Annette pulled him down beside her on the bed.

"What do you think of Mr. Truelove?" she had asked.
"Do you like him?"

"Think of who?"

Turning away from the bear, he looked at her in a puzzled manner.

"That's my teddy's name, Wayne. Mr. Truelove."

He turned to stare once more at the huge black bear with the golden ears and green eyes.

"You like him, don't you, Wayne?" she asked hopefully.

"Well," he began uncertainly, "well, I don't know. What do you do with it? What's it for?"

"Mr. Truelove sleeps with me every night and stays right here all day long waiting for me to come home."

"Why?"

"Because I need him to keep me from feeling lonely." Her face slightly flushed with excitement, Annette began talking rapidly. "If I feel so lonely that it makes me want to cry, I can snuggle up close to Mr. Truelove and put my arms around him and hug him good, and that keeps the nasty old loneliness away."

"What did you name it that for? What's it mean?"

"I named him Mr. Truelove because he loves me all the time and never fails to be right here in my room when I'm lonely and want him close to me."

Wayne took his hand away from her, as he sat up with a stiffening of his body.

"That's sounds silly to me, and if that's how you feel about an old stuffed bear with that silly-looking grin, then you sure don't need me."

"Don't be like that, Wayne," she said anxiously, as a worried smile passed quickly over her face. "I don't want you to be jealous. Mr. Truelove is only a teddy bear. He's not real like you are."

"Well, it's here all day and night, and I'm not."

"Wayne, just as soon as we can be together in our own way, then Mr. Truelove will go to live somewhere else and never come back. Don't you see, Wayne?"

She reached over and touched his hand. "Everything is all right now, isn't it, Wayne?"

He jerked his hand away. "Where did you get that thing?" he said harshly.

"Daddy gave me Mr. Truelove. Daddy went somewhere for him and brought him home to me."

"Why in hell did he do that?" Wayne demanded roughly. He turned and glowered at the huge teddy bear reclining upon the pile of pillows at the head of the bed. "Go on, tell me why. What for, for God's sake?"

"I told Daddy I was going to leave home because Mama was always scolding me about something and finding fault and was so mean to me all the time that I couldn't stand it any longer. Daddy knows how mean to me she can be, how she's always picking on me about little things. He says she has a lot of nervous trouble and we shouldn't blame her too much for the way she acts, and maybe after a while she can get well. But the way it is, she acts like she never wants to get well and would rather stay like she is.

"Daddy said he didn't want me to go away while I was still so young, and to wait till I graduated from high school, and then I could leave home and go to college to study to be a schoolteacher like I want to be, and never have to come back here and be scolded by Mama again. Daddy knows how much I love him and want to do what he tells me. He knew I'd be miserable staying here in the same house with Mama until I graduated from high school. I told him that no matter how much I tried to keep from leaving home, that if she kept on finding fault no matter how much I tried to please her, then I might have to run away.

"That's when Daddy said if I wouldn't go away he'd get me a cuddly life-size teddy bear and a great big wide bed for both of us to sleep in, and whenever Mama fussed too much, I could come get in bed with my teddy bear and cuddle up with him. Mama's still awfully mean to me, but it doesn't matter as much now as it did before Daddy brought me Mr. Truelove."

Wayne was already shaking his head long before she

had finished trying to explain her need for the teddy bear.

"But, Wayne, why are you doing that?" she asked with concern. "Don't you think it's all right? Other girls have teddy bears and things like that for company."

"No, it's the silliest damn thing I ever heard of. Like a grown-up girl playing with dolls and things like that instead of going out on a date and doing things with boys. That's why it's so silly."

"It's no such thing," she protested. "You ought to take back every word of that. The only reason you think that is because you don't know what it's like to be a girl. If you could be a girl for even a few hours, you'd feel the difference and know right away what it's like. Then you wouldn't say such awful things about what a girl needs. All girls want something like Mr. Truelove to cuddle up with when they're lonely and feel unhappy and don't have a real sweetheart for things like that."

"If that's what you want it for, you could hug a pillow just as good."

"A pillow is not a real thing like a teddy bear is."

"Well, I wouldn't want to keep on having anything to do with a girl who liked a stuffed teddy bear more than the real me."

"That's not fair, Wayne." Annette spoke up quickly, her voice rising to a high pitch. "It's not a bit fair to talk like that. I didn't say I liked Mr. Truelove more than I'd ever like a real person. But when there's nobody else——"

"If you want to know how it is with me, I'll tell you," Wayne said, before she could finish what she was saying. "For me, I'd want a girl who'd be a real kissing sweetheart and cuddle up to me and want to do all kinds of things together instead of fooling around with an old dummy of something stuffed with sawdust or rags or whatever's on the inside of that thing you've got."

Tears had already come to Annette's eyes and were starting to run down her cheeks.

"I wish you wouldn't talk like that . . . that way about him. I don't have anybody else—nobody at all. And I need somebody so much. . . ."

Wayne reached for her hand and patted her comfortingly.

"Annette, I didn't mean to make you feel so bad," he said kindly. "But if I'm going to be your sweetheart, then you shouldn't need that thing."

Annette tried to smile through her tears.

"But, Wayne, you know . . . we're too young to marry yet or live together some way. And I promised Daddy I'd finish high school and go to college like he wants me to do. That means I'll be all alone going to bed at night while we're waiting. That's why I want to keep Mr. Truelove. Don't you see, Wayne? He's all I've got when I can't be with you."

Instead of saying anything, Wayne put his arms around her and hugged her tightly against his chest until she was no longer crying. After a while she found one of his hands and drew it close to her and began kissing his fingers one after the other.

Closely embraced on the side of the bed, they had been sitting in silence for a long time in the darkening afternoon when with a click of a switch the room was in dazzling brightness. Unable to see anything at first, Annette recognized immediately the shrill voice of her mother.

"I caught you! And what a disgraceful sight to walk in like this and see with my own eyes! What a shocking thing to see! I hate to believe my own eyes!"

Annette and Wayne had already moved far apart but were still sitting on the same side of the bed.

"Annette! What have you been doing?" her mother demanded in the same shrill voice. "And on that bed with a boy! Say something! Don't you have any shame at all? I don't know what you can say, but I know what it looks like!"

"Mama, we've been talking," Annette answered, speaking as calmly as possible. "That's all. Just talking. And arguing, too, about something. That's all it was, Mama."

"Talking and arguing, huh! And you think I'm going to believe that's all you've been up to? And in this room as dark as it was?"

"Mama, you can believe me. Ask Wayne. He'll tell you the truth, just like I am. Go on and ask him, Mama."

Wayne had got up from the bed and was moving toward the door. But Annette's mother stood in his way.

"Come here, Annette," she said with a beckoning gesture. "Come here and stand in front of me."

"Why, Mama? What for?" she asked as she got up and walked slowly toward her mother. "What do you want?"

Stepping forward, her mother reached down and grasped the hem of Annette's skirt, lifting it to reveal the bareness of her body.

"Look at that nakedness!" her mother was saying as Annette quickly pulled her dress down to conceal herself. "I knew it, I just knew it! You took off your panty-drawers and got on that bed with him and then tried to make me believe you'd been doing nothing. I knew I ought to be suspicious when I caught you and him here in the dark. And now to find out you had your panty-drawers off! What you need is a slapping like you never had in your life!"

"Please don't hurt me, Mama!"

"Shut up and stop trying to beg off after what you've done!"

With a tightening of her lips, Annette's mother lunged forward and struck each side of Annette's face.

"I'm going to tell your father on you," she said. "I'm going to tell him exactly what I found out when I pulled up your dress." She turned and pointed at Wayne. "And now, you! I'm going to tell Annette's father about catching you in here with her. I don't know what he'll do to you, but

I never want to see you inside this house again. And if she gets in trouble because of what you've done to her, I'm going to make it so bad for you that you'll wish you were someone else."

Part THREE

A few days following her seventeenth birthday, Annette graduated from Richland High School. Shortly afterward, Wayne Lombard came home to work for the summer in his parents' variety store. He had finished his second year at Southeastern State University in Plairview, about sixty miles from Richland, where almost all of his courses were in economics and commercial accounting and business management.

Annette had already been accepted at the same university, and by that time was more eager than ever to become a qualified kindergarten teacher. She planned to major in education and take courses in applied teaching during her four years of study at Southeastern State.

It was immediately after her graduation, and several days before Wayne came home, that Annette's father asked her what she intended to do about Mr. Truelove when she left home in the fall to enter the university. That was when he said jokingly that it was probably against the dormitory regulations to sleep with a life-size teddy bear.

Annette had become so strongly attached to the teddy bear during the past two years while Wayne had been away at the university that it was painful for her even to think of leaving it behind or giving it to somebody who would never be able to appreciate Mr. Truelove as she did.

Continuing to talk about the bear in his joking manner, Annette's father had said that his real reason for wanting Mr. Truelove to be placed in a foster home before she left for the university was because it would be an embarrassment to advertise it for sale and then have to bargain and haggle with strangers over the price to be paid for a stuffed teddy bear with the sentimental name of Mr. Truelove.

Wayne had been home from the university for almost a month, and they were walking home late in the evening from a downtown movie, when Annette, speaking light-heartedly, mentioned the teddy bear to him for the first time that summer. What she had in mind was merely to tell him that she and her father had talked about finding a home for it. But suddenly the thought of it made her feel like crying, because she knew she was going to be lonely at the university without Mr. Truelove to sleep with her.

As soon as she had spoken, and with a fervent wish, she hoped her mention of Mr. Truelove would prompt Wayne to say that she ought to live with him instead of with a stuffed teddy bear. Instead, she could feel his body stiffen against her arm.

"I'm sick of all this fuss about a goddamn toy," he shouted.

"Wayne . . ." Annette hesitated.

He refused to look at her.

"Wayne . . . please don't be angry."

She felt a slight movement of his arm.

"I don't want you to be angry—please don't be."

"I can't help it—the whole thing bothers me."

Annette moved closer and looked up at him appealingly. "Wayne . . . Wayne, I wish you wouldn't . . ."

"So you wish *I* wouldn't!" he said with a taunting laugh, jerking his arm away. "That's nice! What about me? Don't you ever think about anybody except yourself? Suppose I wish *you* wouldn't! Have you ever thought of that? Now, let's hear what you have to say!"

"I don't know," she said sadly. "But I'd say anything if only there wouldn't be any more of this awful quarreling."

"If you want to know something, there wouldn't be any quarreling if it weren't for that damn dressed-up sack of sawdust or old rags or something you're always talking about—that thing in a fur suit of clothes with green eyes and a silly goddamn grin. So what do you have to say about that?"

Annette had drawn in her breath; now she let it out slowly.

"Mr. Truelove. . . ."

"You're damn right! Now you're catching on at last. Mr. Truelove! Mr. Truelove!"

"But, Wayne, Mr. Truelove is only . . ."

"Only what?"

"He's only a teddy bear—that's all."

She tightened the grip of her hands on his arm.

"Only a teddy bear! Only a teddy bear! Then if that's what it is, why in hell don't you call it that instead of what you do? Mr. Truelove! And that's not all. You talk to it and try to make it sound like you're talking to a real person instead of a goddamn sack of sawdust."

"But, Wayne," she said quietly, "you understand, don't you? Sometimes when I'm very lonely, and can't be with you, I can think of him being so real that I can shut my eyes and talk to him, and he's not even a make-believe person anymore. That's how real he is to me."

"Why do you try to fool yourself when you know it's only a sack of sawdust, covered with some black fuzz? It doesn't make sense to me—it's not normal. What do you think I'm made of? You act like that damn dummy full of some kind of trash is somebody better than me."

"No, Wayne! Please don't think that!" she pleaded.

"When you were away at college so much of the time and couldn't be here, I always made believe that he—it—you know what I mean . . . well, that he's you. I'd be so awfully lonely here at home without you—when you couldn't be here so I could touch you and feel you. I had to have something close to me when I couldn't have the real you, but you don't ever have to be jealous at all. The way I love you—"

"Jealous! That's the right word! You said it! I'm jealous, and then some. And, believe me, I've got good reason to be jealous, too!"

"You can't say that, Wayne!" Annette protested loudly. "There's been only you when you came home from college, and then, when you were away all the time, it's been only him—Mr. Truelove."

"There you go again!" Wayne was speaking so loudly by that time that he was actually shouting at her and could have been heard the entire length of the block. "It's all I hear! Mr. Truelove! Mr. Truelove!"

"I don't want you to be so upset, Wayne," she said anxiously. "It's all my fault. I'll take back everything I've said."

"If you didn't say it, you wouldn't have to take anything back. Whenever I want to talk to you about something, you have to go and start blabbering about that damn teddy bear. I've had more than enough of that name by now, and I wish you'd shut up about it. Mr. Truelove! Jesus Christ!"

"Wayne, I didn't mean to make you feel so unhappy about . . ." Annette was able to stop herself from repeating the bear's name. Speaking softly then, she tried to hold back the trembling of her voice. "But he's only a teddy, and that's why I was trying to explain how much I need him when I'm so lonely."

Grasping Wayne's hand, she raised it to her face and pressed it lovingly first against one cheek and then upon the other one. After that, she kissed his fingers over and over again.

"You'd better try to explain to yourself exactly what the hell this bear is all about." With an abrupt motion he pulled his hand from her grasp. "I already know all I ever want to hear about that fuzzy son-of-a-bitch."

A man's voice, rough and angry and startlingly loud— even louder than Wayne's had been—was suddenly heard in the night. Looking behind them from the spot where they had paused at the height of their quarrel, they could see a figure in pajamas standing in the dimly lighted door- way of a house.

"I've had enough of your loud talk," the man called out angrily. "It's keeping me awake. I need my sleep at this time of night."

He paused briefly and then went on with his angry con- demnation. "I don't know who you are, and I don't give a damn. But you'd better pay attention to what I'm telling you about. If you folks are married, now screw off and go home where you belong and stay there to do your loud- mouth quarreling where you won't be a nuisance to me. And if you ain't married, go rent yourselves a place to do your quarreling in. I don't care either way, married or not, just make sure you don't never come back stopping right here in front of my house to fuss and quarrel in the middle of the night and keep me from getting my sleep. Like I said, I'm warning you. Now, screw off. I've got a shotgun that shoots buckshot, and I'll pepper your ass with it till you won't be able to sit on it for a month."

In silence they walked quickly down the street after that, holding hands as they started and then putting their arms around each other in order to feel closer together. They stayed that way until they were within sight of Annette's house. It was midnight by then, and there were no lights in any of the houses and not a sound of any kind to be heard. Even the crickets and night birds that had been so noisy earlier in the evening were silent.

As they approached Annette's house, with every step feeling more reluctant to leave each other, they stopped and stood in the shadows, with their arms still around each other. Drawing Annette closer, Wayne affectionately patted her cheeks. Knowing then that he was no longer angry with her, she pressed her body to him as tightly as she could get.

"I've got to tell you something," he said. "I behaved awfully bad back there, and I'm sorry. Real sorry. And I'm never going to talk to you like that again as long as I live. I mean what I say, because I love you so much. And you've just got to believe me when I say I didn't really mean any of it. And you will still love me just the same, won't you . . . sweetness? Please say you will!"

Grasping his hand, she pressed it to her mouth.

"Darling," she said, "you never called me that before— it's so thrilling. I'll never forget—I'll always remember hearing you say it the first time."

"What about the second time . . . sweetness?"

"Oh, darling Wayne, I do love you so much, and I don't ever want us to quarrel again. It's so terrible, and it hurts so much, and it seems like it'll never end. Never mind, soon there won't be anything like that for us to quarrel about, anyway."

"Why, sweetness? What do you mean?"

"Because I'm not going to take that teddy bear with me when I go off to college. That's a promise, Wayne. I'm going to give it away as soon as I can find somebody to take it, or I'll even throw it away to get rid of it right now. I guess I've grown up enough so I won't need it anymore. I've got you for my love, and you mean more to me now than a million teddy bears. When I feel lonely after this, all I'll have to do is think of you and of us together like we are now this minute, and then everything will be all right."

"That's the nicest thing you could say," he told her with a surge of happiness in his voice. "And what else is so nice about it is that you said it without mentioning that bad old name that caused so much trouble whenever I heard it."

Wayne leaned over her and raised her face upward and eagerly kissed her forehead.

"Now I'll tell you something, sweetness. I've got you, too, and I'm going to keep you pretty much in sight from now on so I can look at you while I'm thinking about you."

Annette was carefully fingering one of the buttons on his shirt, as if trying to decide whether to unfasten all the buttons and kiss his bare chest. As in the past, Wayne knew how easily and quickly she could distract him when she was in a sensuous mood, and this time he held her hands with a firm grip until he could finish what he had started to tell her.

"You remember what that man down the street was talking about when he was doing all that shouting awhile ago?" he said. "About our being married—or not married—and that we ought to have a place of our own where we could quarrel all we wanted to in private without disturbing anybody? You remember that, don't you?"

"Yes, of course. Every word. Listening to him yell at us wasn't very pleasant, but I'm glad he said what he did about our needing a place of our own. Don't you feel the same way now, darling?"

"I sure do. I want us to go down to the university and be together and stay together from then on. And if you'll marry me, that'll be really great. And if you don't want to get married that soon, we can start living together just the same—and that'll still be really great. And so now I've asked you to marry me or live with me, and all you have to do is think about it and make up your mind and then let me know which it'll be."

Annette had been listening intently, and at the moment when he finished talking she wrested her hands from his, threw her arms around his neck, and kissed every part of his face that she could reach with her lips.

"Oh, Wayne! You make me so happy. It's the most wonderful feeling I've ever had in my whole life. It makes me want to do anything—everything—for you. All I can think is that I want to kiss all of you all over from head to toe. Tell me what I can do, darling!"

As it had happened before when they became feverish with desire, Wayne grasped the soft flesh of her buttocks with an excited clutching of his hands, while her breasts and thighs pressed closer to him with each surge of her breath.

"You know what I want, sweetness," he said to her.

"Yes, darling," she whispered. "And I do, too."

"But where can we go?"

"We need that place of our own right now."

"I've got a key to the store, and that would be a good place for us," Wayne was saying. "But the trouble is that's so far away, and it would take so much time to go all the way downtown."

The porch light was suddenly switched on with a startling brightness that was like a dazzling sunburst in the night.

"Annette! I know you're out there—I can see you! Don't you try to hide from me!"

Annette's mother, wrapped in a faded brown nightrobe, had come to the porch after turning on the light and was standing at the top of the steps. She was not a large woman, but she was nervous and jerky in her movements, and she had a shrillness of voice that carried the sound of her demands with harsh authority as far as she could be heard. As some of the neighbors had said, it was a pity and a shame that a young girl as charming and pretty as Annette was being raised by a mother who probably should be confined in a rest home or similar institution where she could do no harm.

"You haven't answered me, Annette! Say something!"

"Yes, Mama, I hear you."

"Well, what are you doing out there?"

"We're just standing here. Talking. That's all."

"Don't you know it's after midnight?" her mother said in her scolding manner. "What will the neighbors think of me for raising a daughter who's out there on the street as late as it is? Why don't you have sense enough to come in the house when it's so late? Don't you want to be decent?"

Annette remained silent while she and Wayne watched her mother in the bright light of the porch.

"I know!" she called out in her loud voice. "I can see that Wayne Lombard out there with you. And if you haven't already done it, you're fixing to do some sexing with him. I've told him before, and I've told you a dozen times this summer, for him to stay away from here and quit trying to do what he's after. Are you paying attention to what I'm saying to you, Annette?"

"Yes, Mama," she answered unhappily. "I know what you said. I was listening."

"Come here to me so I can look at you. I want to see if you're wearing all your underclothes."

"Mama, I'm not going to let you do that," Annette protested defiantly. "Now, go away and leave me alone! You have no right to do things like that to me!"

"You shut your nasty-talking mouth! If you say another word like that to me, I'll come out there and slap your face till you're lop-eared! Now, come here like I told you so I can find out what I suspect!"

Only a moment had passed when Annette's father, saying not a word as he suddenly appeared, grasped her mother's arm and took her back into the house. The front door was slammed shut and the porch light was turned off, and then all was quiet in the night.

ANNETTE had often thought of all those years that had gone by so swiftly since that memorable summer night when Wayne Lombard had asked her to marry him and when, after her mother could no longer annoy them, they had gone behind the house for hours of lovemaking that lasted until dawn.

From that time onward there had been such an abundance of happiness for her to enjoy day and night, and so little misery to be endured, that there had been many times during her marriage to Wayne when she felt as if she were utterly selfish and unduly privileged—and even immoral—to have such good fortune in life while so many other married women close to her own age complained so bitterly about their miserable lives.

Beginning with her first year at the university, Annette had often felt uncomfortable among many of the other married students at Southeastern State, who always seemed to have an endless series of gripes and complaints about the meager amount of money provided by stingy parents, the spiteful meddling of officious in-laws, and the irritating enforcement of campus regulations by the university administration.

In addition, it was not unusual for the wives, when safely among themselves, to complain with explicit frankness about the selfish demands and inadequate support, sexual misconduct, and other common failings of their young husbands.

("I was never real sure if I envied Annette or positively hated the sight of her. Right from the beginning, she was so different from the rest of us who married so young—and a lot of times wishing we hadn't. Maybe conceited isn't the right word for it. Anyhow, she was so sure of herself and behaved like she and Wayne Lombard were the only two people in the world who knew what love was all about. It seemed like it made no difference to them to be married or not, because all that mattered was being in love. I don't know where they got their philosophy or logic or whatever methodology they applied to their love life, but seeing them so happy together made me feel like crying my eyes out because of my own miserable life.

("When Tom and I were married and came to the university, I thought it was going to be all super and no drag —like a year-long pizza-party picnic. And was I fooled! The way it turned out was that I could never get the feeling of being truly in love, and Tom didn't want to admit that we'd made a mistake. What he'd say was that we'd have to do a lot more making it before we could appreciate real love. Hell's bells! You can't spend all your time making it!

("I asked some other married girls at the university if they regretted not waiting longer to get married or if they'd do the same all over again. Some of them say it's great to have your own personal bedmate if you can keep yourself fooled that he won't cheat on you in his spare time. Hell's bells! What a way to live! But just look at Annette—married and in love at the same time! To tell the truth, I guess my real feeling about Annette is that I envy her and hate her at the same time.")

Wayne had graduated from Southeastern State two years before Annette received her academic degree and the important certificate that would enable her to teach kindergarten classes in public schools. In order not to live apart while she was completing her four-year course, Wayne had been able to arrange to go to work as an assistant manager of the Plainview branch of a large chain store.

As eager as they were to have their first child, Annette and Wayne had agreed to wait several years before starting the family of three they wanted.

"It's not easy waiting like this for things we want so much to happen," Annette said to Wayne one night when they were in bed. "And right now it's so hard to keep from thinking about them."

She closed her eyes briefly and shook her head as if trying to force forbidden thoughts from her mind.

"And, Wayne . . . it's just as bad when I can't keep from thinking about what might have happened in the past." Catching her breath, she moved closer to him. "Wayne, now when I can reach out and touch you—and feel how fortunate I am—it makes me want to cry when I think what almost happened to me. It would've been so horrible!"

Wayne patted her consolingly.

"But it's all in the past now, Annette, and you don't have to think about it ever again. I don't want you to be upset and unhappy about something that might have happened but actually never did. Please forget all about it."

Tears had come to her eyes, and she was trying to hold back her sobs. Reaching for Wayne's hand, she squeezed it with a desperate grip.

"But I can't forget . . . I don't think I ever will. Even when I'm asleep, I still can't forget. That's when I have those bad dreams in the middle of the night. The last time was such a horrible nightmare."

"I know, Annette. I woke you up when you screamed,

and you told me about it. You said you tried to reach out and touch me and couldn't feel me because I wasn't there. But you know I was here in bed beside you all the time, wasn't I? You remember that, don't you?"

She wiped the tears from her cheeks.

"Yes, Wayne, and I know you're here now, too." Taking a deep breath, she waited until she would be able to speak calmly. "But there're still a lot of times when I'm asleep that I have those bad dreams about what could have happened—and almost did happen, too. And when I wake up in the morning after one of those horrible dreams, I remember it so clearly that I think it just had to be real and wonder if I should tell you about it."

"You've told me about some of your dreams," Wayne reminded her.

"Yes, but not everything—not nearly everything."

"Then go ahead and tell me more. Tell me what bothers you so much and makes you have all those bad times when you are asleep. I want to know, Annette."

"Well, you know all about my mother and the way she treated me and made me want to run away from home. Well, there was a time when I came awfully close to going off with another girl. And it's usually about her and what did really happen and what might've happened that makes me have these bad dreams and nightmares."

"But you don't have to keep on having them. That's all in the past."

"But I can't quit having them, because they remind me that I wouldn't have even known you if I'd gone off from home then. Don't you see, Wayne? We wouldn't be to-gether now like this. That's what makes it so awful to think about, and that's why I keep on having these hor-rible dreams."

"All right, sweetness. What I want you to do now is tell me about this particular girl you mentioned—the one you planned to go away with. What was her name?"

"I'll tell you about it, Wayne. I've got to now. I can't keep it all tied up inside me any longer. I'll tell every word of it if it'll put an end to all these horrible dreams and nightmares."

Annette's voice trembled slightly as she spoke.

"Her name was Jewel Browning. We went to the same school. She was fourteen when I was twelve. Jewel looked a lot older than she really was. And she had such beautiful golden hair—long and thick and wavy. I envied her so much and wanted to be as old as she was and have her kind of hair. Jewel was real pretty, even if she was sort of too chubby from her neck to her hips.

"One day Jewel said she had a secret and would tell it to me if I promised never to tell anybody. I promised, and so Jewel told me she was planning to run away from home and that I could go with her."

"Why did your friend—Jewel Browning—why did she want to leave home?" Wayne asked.

"Jewel said she wanted to go somewhere and learn all about sex so she could become a call girl. When she told me that, I was shocked. It was a big surprise to me. When I asked her why she wanted to be a call girl, she said it was because nobody would ever want to marry her since she was so chubby. But she said being chubby wouldn't keep her from being a good call girl, because it would help to get men interested in her for sex when they saw her unusually large bosom.

"Well, I still wanted to leave home, and Jewel said I wouldn't have to do what she did, she only wanted me to keep her company so she wouldn't be alone when she wasn't working. She said we'd have plenty to eat and a nice place to live and all the clothes we wanted because she knew she could attract men for sex for pay, since her bosom already measured forty inches, even though she was still only fourteen."

"But what happened?" Wayne interrupted. "Why didn't you run away with Jewel Browning?"

"It's such a terrible thing to think about, even after such a long time." A shudder passed through Annette's body as she spoke. "Poor Jewel!"

"But what happened, Annette? Didn't you even get started? Were you too afraid?"

"No, that wasn't the reason—it wasn't being afraid. Both of us were brave enough for that. What happened was, the day before we planned to leave, Jewel and I were walking home together from school and talking about what we were going to do the next day. We were walking along and talking so much and not paying attention to anything else, and then, all at once it happened."

"Now I'm really curious," he told her. "What was it that happened right then?"

"A car—it came around the corner just as we were crossing the street. It came so fast there wasn't time to get out of the way. It ran over Jewel, and I can still hear those screeching brakes. Oh, how horrible it was! Jewel was all crumpled up on the street, and a lot of people were crowding around, and I heard somebody say an ambulance was coming.

"I got down beside Jewel and wiped the blood from her face and brushed her beautiful blond hair from her eyes. One of her legs was all twisted and bent as if it didn't belong to her anymore, and one side of her chest was crushed against the pavement. She was in so much pain that she could scarcely breathe, but she tried to whisper to me, and I could hear some of what she was saying. 'Annette . . . don't run away—don't go off by yourself—there'd be nobody to take care of you. . . . I can't go with you . . . don't run away. . . .'

"The ambulance came then and took Jewel to the hospital with the sound of the siren screaming. I can still hear it when I have nightmares about not being able to reach out and touch you beside me in bed. And what I keep on thinking is that if Jewel Browning had not been run over by that car and hurt the way she was, she and I would have run away from home the next day, and I wouldn't have ever known you at all, and we wouldn't have each other like we do now."

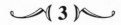

AFTER Annette and Wayne had left Plainview and moved nearly a hundred miles away to a new home in suburban Zephyrfield in the northern part of the state, she said many times during that first year that only a kindly and benevolent fate would have waved a magic wand and brought them such good fortune. However, when she began talking about kindly fate and magic wands, Wayne would merely say that he was too realistic to attribute their good fortune to anything other than sheer blind luck.

"I can't help it, darling," Annette would insist. "Even at my advanced age I still believe in little elves."

"Go right ahead, sweetness," he would say. "I'll keep placing my hunch bets on old-reliable blind luck. By hedging like that, one or the other is bound to pay off."

"But, darling, why can't you believe in magic wands?"

"Because I think I get better odds betting on luck."

At the beginning of his business career with Moneysworth Variety in Plainview, and without Annette being aware of what he was planning, Wayne had carefully outlined a program of living to take place in a systematic manner. It was agreed by the company's regional office that Wayne would be transferred to the Zephyrfield store on a date to coincide with Annette's graduation from Southeastern State University.

It was also understood that certain officers of the company would use their influence and best efforts to try to obtain for Annette a firm commitment for a teaching position in the public-school kindergarten.

When Annette was officially notified of her teaching appointment, it came as a complete surprise to her after all, since the only thing she had done about it was sign a blank application form; she then had said to Wayne that it could only be the waving of a magic wand by little elves that could possibly bring such good fortune. She had a job, she had Wayne. They'd found a comfortable five-room house at the eastern end of Flower Street, where just a few blocks away lived Evelyn and Jack Summerall, with whom they had immediately become friends.

It was at the end of their first year in Zephyrfield when, one evening in summer, sitting on the terrace, Wayne said that the time had come for them to begin making realistic plans for their present and future.

"Darling, do you mean I've got to grow up all at once and stop dreaming about all the wonderful things little elves can do? And just when I was really convinced that I wouldn't have been hired to teach my kindergarteners if there hadn't been a magic wand?"

"This is a good time to mention that," he told her seriously. "Let's start right now being realistic and clarify that situation so you won't be misled and believe you can depend on magic wands to give you what you want in the future. This will have to be harsh, because we live in a harsh world, and I want you to be able to survive in it. Look, Annette, this is the way it was. The teaching job you wanted so much was the result of considerable human persuasion, not waving a stick or other such nonsense. This doesn't mean that I'm not glad I was able to make a present of it to you. I'll always be glad about that."

"Darling, I couldn't help being suspicious, but it was so nice to believe in the magic wand, even though I knew it took more than magic and luck to get the job. Only Wayne Lombard could do all that for me."

"Thanks," he said shortly. "I'm glad you're finally ready to put aside all that nonsense and become a realistic, thinking person."

"I'll think about that," Annette said with a slight frown that slowly turned into one of her pleasant smiles. "Although it may take a little time for my mind to make a complete turnabout on such short notice."

"Good for you," Wayne said in his own serious manner, but still not smiling at her. "I can see that your mind is at work, and I consider that to be a favorable sign."

"Thanks for the encouragement, darling," she replied quickly. "That's exactly what I was doing. Thinking, and thinking hard. And since you are banishing all magic from our kingdom, I was wondering if you mean for us to be prudent and realistic all the time, including Sundays and legal holidays."

"Of course."

"Well, Mr. Realistic, in that case, may I sit on your lap while I do some serious thinking?"

"No."

"What did you say?"

"No!"

"But, darling, if I can't sit on your lap, what will I do when I stop thinking and am just sitting here?"

"I'll tell you," Wayne said. "When you're ready to be serious about a serious matter, then we can talk about being prudent and realistic and anything else that's necessary."

"Mr. Prudent—I can feel all over me that I want to be serious. Now, may I sit on your realistic lap?"

"No."

"Why can't I?"

Annette was sitting in a chair on the other side of the terrace table, and Wayne was so far away and the table was so wide that she could not lean close enough to be able to kiss him. With an exaggerated and fretful pouting, she picked up a magazine from the table and rolled it up tightly and began kissing it over and over again as if she were kissing his hand.

She was still pouting when she hurled the magazine aside and leaned as close to Wayne as she could get.

"You didn't answer me at all just now when I asked you if I could sit on your lap," she said. "Why won't you let me do that . . . Mr. Prudent . . . Mr. Realistic . . . Mr. Lombard?"

"Sweetness, it's not that I don't want—"

"Then what is the reason?"

"Well, it's like this. When you sit on my lap, it has a way of leading from one thing to another, none of which has anything to do with what we're trying to discuss seriously."

"Is that so bad, darling?"

"Well, it's not so good when we're trying to talk about our personal and financial affairs."

"And after all that has been taken care of . . . ?"

Wayne smiled at her across the table.

"That's an easy question to answer, sweetness. Then it'll be permissible and logical for us to let lap-sitting lead from one thing to another."

"Come on," she said. "Let's call this business meeting to order so I can make a motion for adjournment. Now, just what is it exactly that we're going to be very realistic about?"

"There are four items on the agenda, and these can be described as the four important phases of our future." Wayne spoke with a calm briskness, as if he had carefully rehearsed what he was to say to her. "Now, I'll name these phases in the order in which I think they should be considered and put into operation. They are all of equal importance in our lives. What I mean is that we want to plan for first things first, second things second, and so on in that sequence. Is this clear?"

"One, two, and so on. I think I know how to keep score."

On the hillside beyond the terrace, house lights could be seen on the eastern slope, twinkling cozily in the summer warmth all the way from the top of the ridge down to the bottom at Flower Street.

"I heard what you said about keeping score, Annette," Wayne said abruptly. "Just remember that a little flippancy will go a long way. And don't forget that none of this can be accomplished without your cooperation—and a consistently serious attitude on your part. Now, I want to say that your suggestions are needed, and I want you to speak up and say what you think about the program I'm working on for us. So if you've been listening . . ."

"Darling, I'm listening with both ears while waiting patiently for the lap-sitting to begin—and not forgetting what you hinted that might lead to."

"Well, you'd better pay attention to what I'm saying so that if I ask you a question or need your comment . . ."

"If you do ask me a question, do you want to know what I hope you'll ask me?"

"What?" he said in a cautious manner.

"Darling, I hope you'll want to know when I think the lap-sitting should start."

"Don't worry," he said shortly. "When I want to know that, I know who to ask."

"Wayne," she said, lowering her voice and speaking to

him with a provocative softness, "Wayne, darling, do you remember what you used to say when we were first married and you wanted me to sit on your lap?"

"No," he answered with a pretended brusqueness. "I don't remember now, but some other time . . ."

"I haven't forgotten, darling. You used to say that to the best of your knowledge I had the softest goosey-downy bottom in the whole world."

"All right, all right! I heard that, Annette!" Wayne had spoken sternly. However, he was unable to keep from smiling at her momentarily. "Now, if you'll pay attention . . ."

"Darling, don't you still think so—about my having the softest goosey-downy—"

"Never mind, Annette! Now, here's number one on the agenda, and it's very important for you to know about it. I'm arranging to take out triple insurance coverage on my life, with you as sole beneficiary. In the event of my early death, the sum of money you would receive will be ample enough to pay all debts and establish a sizable trust fund that will take care of you very comfortably as long as you live. Now, as I said, that's the number-one item, or phase."

Annette, unobserved by Wayne in the faint light while he was speaking so earnestly, had unfastened her dress and was carefully pushing it downward over her hips. When the dress dropped to the terrace floor, she quickly kicked it under the table.

"Now, for the next phase, the number two on the agenda," Wayne went on in his brisk, businesslike manner. "I'm starting at once to earmark and set aside in a separate account at the bank as much money as we'll be able to save monthly out of income. The purpose of this fund will be to use it as a down payment for a home of our own that will be larger and much better than this make-shift rented house we're living in now. It'll be something more suitable in size for a family of five persons. And if you're wondering why I said we need a large house for five persons when there are only two of us at present, that'll be explained in the item to follow."

By that time, Annette had taken off not only her dress but also everything else she had been wearing and was sitting there calmly in the dim light watching Wayne on the other side of the terrace table.

"Am I making all this clear, Annette?"

"Every syllable of it, darling."

"Fine, fine," he remarked hurriedly, nodding to himself. "I'm glad to hear that. And now we come to number three, the matter of our planning for the three children we've talked so much about in the past. The way I see it working out, as far as our finances are involved, and taking into consideration the money needed for the life-insurance program, savings for the down payment on the magnificent home we're going to have, and putting money aside for emergencies and so forth . . . well, I've figured that in a couple of years from now, even if I don't get any more salary raises or another bonus from Moneysworth Variety, we'll be in good shape. You can retire from your teaching and begin populating our own personal kinder-garten at home. You've said many times that's what you want to do, raise three children, and now it's going to be possible at last. So, sweetness, what do you think of that—item number three?"

Annette had thought she would be able to attract Wayne's attention by purposely remaining silent, but after she had waited quite a while and he still had not looked in her direction, she finally got up and went to the other side of the table and stood beside him.

As close as she was to Wayne, he was too preoccupied to notice what she had done until she sat down on his lap and his hands felt the warmth of her bare body.

"Remember me?" she said teasingly as she saw him staring at her in surprise.

"I'll bet you were too busy getting undressed to pay any attention to what I was trying to tell you."

Nevertheless, he tightened his arms around her and kissed her eagerly. Finally she straightened up on his lap and held his face in her hands.

"I heard all you said, darling. Every word of it. Now, I'm curious about what you haven't told me yet. You said there were four phases, or items, on the agenda, and you've told me only three of them so far. I know, because I've been very careful about keeping score. What is number four, darling?"

Wayne was evasive. "Not now, sweetness," he said. "Let's skip it tonight. And don't worry. Some other time will be soon enough to talk about it."

"But if it's important, why do we have to wait?"

"Well, for one thing . . . it's getting late."

"If that's the way it's going to be, I don't think I ought to agree to cooperate till I know what the fourth item is."

"Let's forget it. This isn't the right time and place. Besides, right now, well, you know what happens when you take off your clothes and sit with your goosey-downy bottom on my lap."

"I know, darling. One thing leads to another."

Getting up then and carrying her in his arms, Wayne took her down the dark hall to their room.

EVEN though she had already endured several weeks of devastating anguish since Wayne's death and burial, Annette was still far from being able to recover from the shock of what had happened.

She couldn't believe that Wayne was actually no longer living, or make herself realize that he was not away from home on a business trip and would soon return. At night she would wake up and reach for him, pathetically calling his name when she could not feel his warm, muscular body beside her in bed.

("That was a tragic thing to happen as it did. Annette and Wayne were so young, and such a devoted couple. Aside from the personal tragedy of being widowed, her great desire to have children will never be fulfilled now. Perhaps it's for the best. She's sweet and beautiful, but childlike herself, and very unstable. Wayne's death seems to have made her more unbalanced than ever, and of course, her future is uncertain at this point. I just don't know what's going to happen to Annette, though. Evelyn Summerall says she wants to continue teaching kindergarten. Annette is still so young and beautiful, I can't see her being content to teach school for the next twenty years instead of remarrying. There are a lot of available men in and around Zephyrfield, and I wouldn't be surprised to see the beginning of considerable action any day now. As you can judge by my interest in her future, I'm very fond of Annette, and I sincerely hope something really good will happen to her.")

The early weeks of unfamiliar widowhood and its tormenting cruelty had passed, but the sorrow and loneliness of Annette's life had continued to inflict misery upon her, and she felt that the only person in Zephyrfield she could trust to be helpful and sympathetic was Evelyn Summerall.

Evelyn had already visited Annette many times since Wayne Lombard's death, and she continued doing everything she could to comfort her. In addition to being genuinely sympathetic, Evelyn felt that she had a practical understanding of how distressed Annette was to find herself suddenly alone in the world after the many years since she had known Wayne. Consequently, Evelyn had been spending as much time as she could with Annette, trying to help her adjust to life without Wayne.

It still had not been conclusively determined what the actual circumstances were at the time of Wayne Lombard's death. The police had said that further investigation would have to be made before it could be definitely determined as to how and why he had been killed. It seemed probable, according to the police, that Wayne had been shot to death accidentally while being held up and robbed, or that he had been shot intentionally for attempting to resist the robber's demands, or that he had been killed by a deranged person who took delight in inflicting pain and witnessing death.

Regardless of how Wayne's death came about, however, he had died instantly on the pavement in front of the Moneysworth Variety store in Zephyrfield. This had happened shortly after the six-o'clock closing hour, when he had locked the door for the night after all the clerks and salespeople had left and he was ready to start homeward himself. The police had established the fact that none of the store's money was missing and that the only money the killer could have taken would have been the small amount, perhaps ten or twenty dollars, that Annette had said Wayne ordinarily carried in his pocket.

Ever since the funeral, Annette's grief had been so intense and personal that she had not only kept the doors of her house closed and locked but also, in addition to maintaining that seclusion behind unopened curtains, she had refused to answer telephone calls of well-meaning condolences.

Evelyn Summerall was the only person in Zephyrfield whom Annette would see while she remained in seclusion following the funeral.

Evelyn frequently brought food to the house, and after preparing a meal, would sit with Annette in the darkened room, trying to be as comforting as possible under such gloomy and mournful circumstances.

After one of her visits to Annette, several weeks after Wayne Lombard's death, Evelyn had gone home realizing that Annette, consciously or unconsciously, was troubled about a personal matter that was related in some manner to her late husband. After thinking about it for a time, it was Evelyn's conclusion that Annette, for her own peace of mind, must talk to someone about whatever it was that was obviously disturbing her. Evelyn decided then to go back the next day and try to find out what it could be that had caused Annette to be subjected to a whole new phase of anxiety and worry.

Evelyn knew that Wayne had made ample provision for all of Annette's financial needs in later life with his insurance program. Consequently, other than having to bear the tragic loss of her husband when both of them were so young and so much in love, Evelyn could not think of anything else to make Annette so upset.

When she arrived at Annette's house the following afternoon, Evelyn was surprised when she was greeted so promptly and with extraordinary eagerness at the door.

She was even more surprised to receive from Annette an unexpected hug and kiss.

As if to show how grateful and pleased she was to have Evelyn in her house, Annette kept her arm entwined in Evelyn's as she led her through the dark hallway to the sitting room in the rear of the house.

"Evelyn, there's something very important I've just got to tell you," Annette began as soon as they had sat down. "I'm so glad you're here, so we can talk. You're so wise and understanding—and I need you very much!"

Even though the tone of her voice was serious and exacting, and her hands twisted nervously in her lap, Annette's pale face for the first time in those many weeks of mourning brightened with a brief and gleaming smile. Her flowing brown hair had been brushed to a shining glow, and she was wearing one of her most becoming dresses.

"Of course, Annette. I want to be helpful. Please don't hesitate to—"

"Evelyn, all this time I've tried to keep from thinking about it," she interrupted with a hasty flow of words, "but now I realize how wrong it would be to keep on like this any longer. The horrible nightmares one after the other, the awful lonesomeness of living and not caring if I stayed alive another minute—now it's different, because I've made up my mind about doing exactly what Wayne told me he wanted me to do."

"If that's the way you feel, Annette, I'm sure you'll be doing the right thing. Do you want to tell me about it now?"

"The way it was, Wayne kept on trying to get me to make a promise, and I kept putting it off and wouldn't, and now it's too late for him to hear it. Now, I know I'd hate myself the rest of my life if I didn't do what he wanted me to promise. I will do it! I will do it! You heard me say that, didn't you, Evelyn? Now I've made my promise, just as Wayne wanted me to do, and you heard me! And you'll help me keep my promise, won't you, Evelyn? Please say you will!"

Annette had been talking so rapidly and excitedly that she was gasping for breath. She leaned back in her chair for a moment and closed her eyes. Evelyn had no idea what Annette was talking about, but she wanted to be helpful.

"You can count on me to do anything I can, Annette," Evelyn said gently.

"I don't know what I'd do if it weren't for you now, Evelyn. You're the only friend I've got in the whole world. I'm all alone, with Daddy dead and my mother in a sanatorium for the rest of her life. There's nobody except you now, Evelyn. Please say you're going to help me!"

Hurriedly getting up from her chair and going across the room, Evelyn took Annette into her arms with a close embrace. Almost at the same moment, both of them began weeping unrestrainedly.

It was late in the afternoon when Annette had stopped crying and could smile gratefully at Evelyn.

"I feel so much better now, and I'm going to be all right. You've been so wonderful to me, Evelyn. And I want you to know that I appreciate so very much everything you've done."

"I'm glad I could do something to help when I knew the suffering you had to endure. Now I want to do what I can about the promise you've been so concerned about."

Annette was silent, trying to keep from crying again, and Evelyn leaned closer and patted her arm comfortingly until she was able to speak.

"Now I can tell you about the promise," Annette said with a slight trembling of her lips. "Wayne said in case anything happened to him while I was still young and we had no children at the time of his death—you see, he was always so concerned about me and my desire for children —well, he tried to get me to promise to marry again right away so I could have the children I've always wanted and looked forward to taking care of and raising. Wayne understood so well what little children meant to me. I began playing with dolls when I was very young, and I slept with a big teddy bear named Mr. Truelove, and I liked being a baby-sitter for mothers, and I always wanted to be a kindergarten teacher. And most of all, as Wayne knew, I wanted children of my own. I don't expect anybody else to be like Wayne, but now I've promised myself to do what he wanted, and, as Wayne would say, use my very best efforts. But I don't know how. You must help me, Evelyn! Help me to keep my promise!"

Part FOUR

❧ 1 ❧

THE rough bark of the oak tree where Annette was standing had become cold and wet, and it no longer felt friendly to her touch. Darkness was creeping steadily closer in the drizzle of the night, and the misty glow of lights in nearby houses on both sides of Flower Street appeared to be rapidly receding into the distance.

Annette was increasingly aware of how dangerous it was for a woman to risk walking alone on such a dimly lighted street.

She was still not certain whether she had actually heard Doan speak to her and had really spoken to him, or whether she had imagined it.

"Doan?" she said anxiously, speaking in a faint voice. "Doan? Are you there somewhere? Can you see me?"

She held her breath expectantly as long as she could before speaking again.

"Doan? Didn't you hear me, Doan? Why don't you answer me? Why don't you say something now?"

The sound of her voice was little more than a cautious whisper.

After waiting and listening, and there was still no answer, she began to wonder what would happen to her if she needed him to protect her and he did not come to help her.

"Doan! Doan!" she called loudly into the darkness. This time the frantic gasping of her voice sounded as if her life depended upon hearing him speak to her at that precise moment. Urgently, she called him again, hearing her voice like a scream in the night. "Doan. Oh, Doan!"

Sinking to her knees on the damp earth, Annette locked her arms around the trunk of the oak tree. Her face was pressed so tightly against the rain-wet, rough bark that she could feel a painful pressure on her skin, and her whole body was soon shaking convulsively with the sobs that would not be held back any longer.

As her sobs lessened, Annette began to whisper as though she were talking to another person.

"It's so dark and cold, and I'm so afraid to be here like this and not be able to get to Evelyn Summerall's house. Somebody might be out there watching me—Doan might be doing that right now—they might not let me go where Evelyn is. But it's so dark, and I'm so scared. I can't tell what's real and what's only imaginary. But I know I'm not going back to live with Doan—that's real and not imaginary—because I'm running away. I've wanted to run away from home so many times, and now I've got the best reason in the world. Doan's not like Wayne. I don't love him. He won't let me have the children that Wayne wanted me to promise to have, and I just can't keep on living without having them for Wayne's sake.

"Wayne! I can talk to you now. I know you can hear me. I feel so close to you. You know why I can't stay with Doan any longer. I did what you wanted me to do—marry somebody while I was still young. Evelyn Summerall arranged that. I thought Doan would take your place, and I wanted him to be like you in every way. I even counted on the children I'd have being like you.

"Wayne! Listen to me! I found out I couldn't love Doan. Even if he'd let me have some children now, I still couldn't love him. I still love you and always will. Maybe I can find somebody who looks like you, who reminds me of you so much that it'll be almost real. That's what I want, Wayne! You understand. I know you do. I'm so glad now I can go away and leave Doan."

Suddenly, over the sound of rainwater dripping from the trees, she was sure she could hear Doan's familiar voice speaking to her from the darkness. Knowing his voice so well, his way of talking to her, she thought what she heard had to be real and not imaginary. As she pressed herself closer to the tree, she wondered if he had heard her whispering to Wayne.

"Annette, tell me the truth. Why do you want to leave me? Haven't I been good to you? Don't you know I love you?"

"It doesn't matter. Nothing makes any difference now."

"But there has to be a reason. What is it?"

"You know what you told me."

"About having a baby?"

"Of course!"

"Well, what's wrong with that? Why should I have to populate the world? Can't you rid yourself of this obsession that's ruining our lives?"

"That's one reason why I married you. So I could have children. Three of them. I need them. I can't explain it any other way. Wayne said he wanted me to promise; he said—"

"Wayne! Wayne Lombard! I've had enough of hearing that name. Can't you get him out of your mind and keep him out?"

"No," Annette replied at once.

"Why not?" Doan said in a demanding way.

"Because I loved Wayne."

"But that was when he was living."

"And I'm still in love with him."

"With a dead man?"

"Yes."

"Annette, you can't really mean that."

"I mean it as much now as I ever did, and I always will."

"For God's sake, Annette, he's dead . . . gone . . . buried in the ground! Be normal and think about living in the present—us, me and you. You've had enough of this mourning. And I'll tell you one more thing. I've had enough, and I don't want to hear any more talk about Wayne Lombard again."

"And you won't, either!" she hissed. "Now, go away and leave me alone, Doan Thurmond! It's all so hopeless and cruel. It's foolish to keep on pretending any longer. The make-believe is over and finished. I don't love you, and I don't want you to love me."

"Annette, tell me just one thing."

"What do you want to know?"

"Why did you wait so long to tell me this?"

"I waited as long as I could to find out if you were going to change your mind about a certain matter."

"I understand. You don't have to explain anything. And if you're so determined to have those children you keep on talking about, do you want a divorce right away so you can marry again?"

"That might not be necessary."

"Why not?"

"I won't know anything about it till I see Evelyn Summerall and find out from her what she decides I ought to do."

⚞ 2 ⚟

STILL unable to decide if the familiar voice she had been hearing was really Doan's or if she had merely imagined it, Annette began to shiver. She knew it was very dangerous to be out on the street alone after dark when there had been so many reports of violence in that section of the suburb in recent months. She wondered if a man—Doan? —would leap out of the darkness and grab her if she got up from her knees and tried to run all the way across town to Evelyn's house at the eastern end of Flower Street.

("As time goes on, I've often wondered how much of a favor it was to Annette the way Evelyn Summerall acted as matchmaker to promote her marriage to Doan Thurmond. Everybody knows it was expertly managed and could have been accomplished as smoothly as it was only by a person like Evelyn Summerall. We all know that Evelyn has always been a dedicated do-gooder, and this was to be her all-time good deed. However, the way things are only a few months after the wedding, you can hardly call the marriage a success.

("I don't like to criticize, but I just can't be convinced that Evelyn, with her hobby of casting horoscopes and studying the signs of the zodiac—and reading palms, too— is qualified enough to give anybody advice about marriage. She was so eager to arrange a marriage for Annette that she ignored what many people in Zephyrfield know about Doan Thurmond. Long before Annette appeared on the scene, I heard Doan say on several occasions that his career as a lawyer would be his consuming interest for many years to come and that he was not going to be handicapped early in life by raising a tribe of children.

("He said he would like to marry soon, provided he could find a girl talented enough to be his hostess, and beautiful enough to satisfy his ego. But effective precautions would be the rule of the bedroom, so there would be no danger of children arriving in years to come. Evelyn certainly knew about this prohibition—but then, I've always been a little suspicious of Evelyn Summerall's motives and sincerity. Poor Annette! I feel so sorry for her. I don't know what's going to happen when she finds out the truth about Doan's attitude about children—but I have the feeling that she might do something very drastic.")

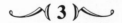

THE misty rain had almost stopped falling by the time Annette had summoned the courage to leave her hiding place behind the oak tree. She had gone as far as the sidewalk when the headlights of an automobile parked at the curb were suddenly switched on and completely blinded her with their dazzling brightness—as if someone in the car had known exactly where she was hiding and was waiting for her to come out of the darkness behind the tree. Could it be Doan?

As her vision gradually returned, however, Annette

could see that the car, an old sedan with splashes of gray mud on the faded brown paint, did not belong to Doan.

Relieved to know that he was not there, she started walking rapidly eastward on Flower Street toward Evelyn Summerall's house on the other side of town.

As she passed the old sedan, she was startled by the appearance of the strange man who was leaning as far as he could out of the window and watching her closely. Even in the faint glow of the street light at the end of the block, and with only a hurried glance at him, Annette knew she would never forget the way he looked.

He appeared to be forty or forty-five years old and had a round chalky-white face with small squinting eyes. Partly bald-headed, with a slight fringe of tannish hair that was almost the same color as the faded paint on his car, he had a heavy tan moustache that was untrimmed and so droopy that it completely covered his mouth. As much as anything else to remember him by, though, was his eye-striking bright-blue shirt with a sheen that would practically glow and shimmer in the dark.

Annette had taken only a few steps when she heard the man's voice.

"Hey, you!" he called to her. "Come back here, and I'll give you a ride to where you're going to. How about it?"

Looking straight ahead, and saying not a word, she began walking faster toward the street light at the corner.

"Hey, you! I want to know something!" His voice then was louder and more commanding. "What you been hiding from back there behind that big tree for? Looks like you've been scared about something. What's the matter with you? You don't say nothing!"

Panicked by the thought of what she would do if he got out of his car and came after her, Annette began to run.

"Hey, you! I'll be looking for you," he called out. "You might decide to change your mind next time."

Annette reached the end of the next block and paused

for breath just as a patrol car with the prominent markings of the Zephyrfield police department suddenly appeared without warning and rolled slowly to a stop at the curb where she was standing.

Her first thought was that Doan had come home, and not finding her in the house, had called the police department and asked that a search be made for her as a missing person. She must get away as quickly as possible and find a safe hiding place.

However, the tall young policeman had already left the patrol car and stood directly in front of her.

"Are you in trouble, miss?" he asked politely.

The brilliant blueness of his eyes was almost the exact color of Wayne's eyes.

"Maybe you didn't hear what I asked you, miss," he said when Annette did not answer. "Are you having some kind of trouble?"

She shook her head.

He was so tall that she had to look up in order to see his face, and so young that Annette wondered if he could actually be old enough to be on the police force. The longer she gazed at him, the more she realized that he looked very much as Wayne had at the same age.

Now that she had seen how blue his eyes were, Annette could not keep from comparing the young policeman's blond hair with almost the same shade of color that Wayne's hair had been. She was still admiring him when she heard him speaking to her again, and she felt a warm flush come to her cheeks.

"Well, miss, if everything is all right, I'd like to know why you're out on a rainy night all alone like this. Are you sure everything is all right? You look pretty wet."

Annette glanced down at her wrinkled, damp dress.

"I know, it looks awful. If that's all, I want to go now," she told him.

With a slight movement, he stood in her way.

"I've got a hunch I ought to check out this situation a little more thoroughly before you go," he said, looking down at her with a slight frown. "I don't know what it'll add up to, but it's not good for a young woman like you to be out all alone like this at night. You've probably heard that there have been some acts of violence on Zephyrfield streets. A couple of women were murdered recently. The police department wants to protect you, and I hope you'll cooperate with us."

Annette nodded. "What do you want me to do?"

"To start with, just for the record, tell me where you came from and where you're going."

"I'm on my way to see a friend."

"Boyfriend or girlfriend?"

Annette ignored his question.

"All right," he said, "it's none of my business. But if you could give me some . . ."

"I'm going to the east end of Flower Street."

"That's about a dozen long blocks from here. Quite a distance for you to walk. Where do you live?"

"Do I have to tell you that?"

He looked at her closely with a questioning frown.

"Never mind," he told her. "We'll come back to that later. Now, tell me about that man you were talking to on the street awhile ago. You know who I mean, the one in the brown sedan parked in the next block."

"I don't know anything about him," she said. "I didn't speak to him at all. He spoke to me."

"What did he say?"

"He wanted me to get into his car with him."

"And you didn't want any of that?"

She quickly shook her head. "No."

"Have you ever seen him before tonight?"

"No. Never."

"Did he offer you money to go with him in his car?"

"No! No!"

This time the policeman smiled—Wayne's smile.

"Well, I'll say this for you," he told Annette. "You were smart not to have anything to do with him. The police department has been tailing him off and on for several months trying to get something on him. Whatever he's doing, he's a slick operator. We haven't been able to get him on even a minor traffic violation. Whatever his game is, it's a little bit more than just driving around town at night and looking at the sights. We know his name and where he lives and what job he sometimes works at, but so far that's just about the limit of our information on him."

He paused, looking at her for several moments, as if reluctant to let her leave.

"Well, miss," he said awkwardly, "I guess I'd better be going. And . . . er . . . please accept my apology for delaying you like this on your way to visit your friend."

With a bow to Annette, and a quick smile, he got into the patrol car, waving his hand in a friendly gesture to indicate that she was free to continue on her way.

ANNETTE had gone only a short distance when she saw the patrol car parked a little ahead of her. The same young officer got out and came up to her. She looked up at him in surprise, a tingle of pleasure running through her body.

"I'm sorry to bother you again, miss, but what happened was—"

"That's all right," she was quick to tell him. "I don't mind at all."

"I've just been through to the desk sergeant at headquarters. He said he wants a full report about this situation. I hope you won't mind answering a few more questions."

Taking a notebook and pencil from his pocket and making motions with the pencil, he was soon concentrating on the task at hand as seriously as if he had been preparing a citation for a traffic violation.

"Your name, please," he asked, making several flourishing motions with the pencil.

"Do you have to know?"

"It would be helpful. And nice to know, too. Mine's Carl."

Annette leaned forward enough to see that the notebook he had been using was an ordinary drawing pad, on which he had already drawn a quick sketch of her face and bosom and flowing brown hair.

She was so pleased that he had wanted to draw the picture of her that she was on the verge of reaching out to grasp his hand and kiss his fingers when he turned and tossed the drawing pad into the patrol car.

"Have you decided yet if you're going to tell me your name?" he asked. "I'm not going to try to guess it."

She nodded with no hesitation. "Annette."

"That's a pretty name, as pretty as you are. But it can't be all. You have to have one more to put beside it."

He waited for her to say something, but she remained silent.

"Well, Annette, I can't order you to show me your driver's license for complete identification. You are a pedestrian and are not operating a motor vehicle. You're not even on a bicycle or roller skates. By the way, do you ever go roller-skating?"

"No," she said.

"It's very good exercise—much better for you than push-ups and athlete's foot and Sunday driving. If you tried it once, you might find that you liked it so much you'd become a roller-skating fanatic—or a fanatic on roller skates, if you want to say it that way."

Annette, smiling slightly, had been shaking her head.

"All right, Annette," Carl said as he took his police report forms from his pocket, "we didn't get very far on roller skates. So back to the business at hand. The sergeant down at headquarters is going to start squawking any minute now on that radiophone with his mouth full of static, and he'll want all the facts about you. And by the way, the desk sergeant's name is Roy Royal. And it's a shame to waste a name like that on a fat-faced police sergeant when it could be used to make a big star out of a nightclub comedian or country singer. But that's something else. What I need to know now is your home address. Where do you live, Annette?"

"Fifteen-fifteen Flower Street."

Carl repeated the address aloud as he made the notation on his pad.

"That's not far from here. Just about two or three blocks. I know where it is. It's the home of Mr. Thurmond. Doan Thurmond, the lawyer."

He looked up inquiringly at Annette.

"Do you live there, or work there, or what?"

She nodded as he spoke.

"But you're not saying which or what," he said to her in a slightly scolding tone. "And this makes me curious. You could be Mrs. Thurmond. But why would Doan Thurmond's wife be out on the street alone at this time of night getting wet in a drizzle without a raincoat or umbrella? You said your name is Annette, and you live at the Doan Thurmond address, but do you live there for love or money? If you're not going to do any explaining, I'm

going to call in and ask the sergeant if there's an appre-
hend-and-hold order out for a runaway white female who
doesn't look a day over thirty and who . . ." He stopped
abruptly. "I mean, not over twenty-one."

"Please don't do that!" Annette begged. "Please let me
leave—don't keep me here like this!"

But Carl was already speaking on the radiophone, and
he waved his hand for her to be silent.

"She doesn't look a day over twenty-one, Sergeant,
and she has long brown hair hanging down her back all
the way to where she can sit on it. Honest, she does. I'm
not joking, Sergeant. And she's really good-looking—if
you can afford the brunette type and are not too deep in
debt to a blonde on the side. She's close to five-feet-four,
and just the right cuddly weight to be barefoot and hitch-
hiking through your mind about five-fifteen in the morning,
when you suddenly sit up in bed and reach for her. And
spend the next hour wondering where she went to. Now,
if that's not enough, and you need some additional descrip-
tion—"

Carl was interrupted by the officer at police headquarters, who asked if the person under surveillance was
actually a barefoot female hitchhiker.

"Sergeant, the fact is that this is a good-looking chick
with shoes on. She could be anybody's sweetheart—I
think. But let's check her out good. She might be a nice
girl who sawed a couple of guys in half with her electric
saw or will trigger her double-barreled handgun if she's
in a hurry. You told me not to forget that it's always the
good-looking chicks and never the ugly dames who get
maddest the fastest and shoot the straightest and the
quickest. Now you know what I know, Sergeant. Just
tell me if you want me to bring her down to headquarters
or let her go."

"What's her name, Carl?" he asked.

"Annette."

"I want the full name."

"That's all she'll tell me, and I'm too much of a gentle-man—"

"You shouldn't keep me here like this," Annette protested. "And talk about me the way you've been doing. You have no right to do this to me—I haven't done anything to make me be treated like this. It's not fair at all."

"Fair or not, what I'm thinking is that I ought to contact Mr. Doan Thurmond and find out if anybody is missing at his house. If somebody is missing, he could be worried out of his mind by now."

"No, Carl!" she pleaded urgently. "Don't do that! Let me go—let me go!"

"If it bothers you that much, I won't contact Mr. Thurmond, unless you've been reported missing, and we'll know about that very soon now. And I'm pretty sure that the sergeant at headquarters is going to say you can go free. But you might as well know that I've done all this on purpose. I wanted to keep you here as long as I could so I could talk to you, and it was the only excuse I could use. I hope you won't hold that against me too much, Annette. I think you're wonderful."

Trembling, Annette had moved closer to Carl, knowing that more than anything she wanted to put her arms around his neck and kiss him. Tears came to her eyes as she looked up at him.

"Carl, are you married?"

"Yes. Very much so."

"Do you have any children?"

"I sure do. Three."

"Three!" she exclaimed loudly. "That's what I want!"

"Then why not?"

"He won't let me. But you're so much like somebody else, and . . ."

"What do you mean by that, Annette?" he asked, looking into her eyes.

"I don't know . . . I don't know! I'm so desperate! And even if I could have only just one—"

There was a noisy crackling of static on the radiophone, and Carl hurried to the patrol car to answer the call. The desk sergeant, speaking crisply, directed him to investigate immediately the reported robbery of a small food market many blocks away on the north side of Zephyrfield. When Carl asked about a report on Annette, he was told to forget it and to hurry across town to the scene of the holdup.

"Annette, I've got to leave you now," he told her hastily. "I wish I didn't have to hurry away and leave you here like this."

Reaching for his hands, she excitedly kissed each of his fingers over and over again, the tears running down her cheeks.

"Annette," she could hear Carl say, "I want you to stop at the first house you see and ask to use the phone to call a taxi or your friend or somebody. I don't want you staying on the street alone a minute longer. It's too dangerous. Will you promise me, Annette?"

"Yes, I promise, Carl," she said earnestly, trying to hold back her sobs. "I'll do that. I'll do anything you want me to do, Carl!"

Part FIVE

◝❮ 1 ❯◜

THE cold springtime drizzle of the late afternoon had gradually stopped falling during the past hour, and the change in the weather had brought a thick gray fog that already was beginning to obscure the treetops and was slowly settling down close to the damp pavement. In the grayness, Flower Street appeared to be even more deserted and lonely than during the earlier rainfall.

Annette had gone almost the whole length of the block after Carl had driven away so abruptly in the patrol car, and remembering so clearly his concern for her safety when he had to leave her, she had been glancing cautiously over her shoulder after every few steps to see if she were being followed by somebody.

Presently, with one of her backward glances she did see, coming slowly behind her, less than a block away, the dim beams of automobile headlights that were barely able to penetrate the thick gray fog.

Her immediate thought was terrorizing. Doan had arrived home from his office, and discovering that she had left the house, had come looking for her on the street, and now had seen her.

Darting in haste from the sidewalk, Annette crouched

behind a clump of bushes on somebody's lawn. Clutching her damp yellow dress tightly around her and hoping she could not be seen where she was trying to hide, she wondered if she had been fortunate enough to be able to get out of sight before being seen.

As she waited tensely, breathing quickly and shivering with the touch of rain-drenched bushes on her face and arms, the automobile moved slowly and almost silently along the street only a short distance from her. As close as she was, though, she was not able to see in the gray fog if Doan or somebody else was driving the car. Just the same, the large dark-green sedan did look familiar to her, and after that she felt certain that it was Doan's car and that he was looking for her.

"Oh, dear God, please don't let Doan find me," she whispered in a voice so faint that she could barely hear it herself. "Oh, dear God, don't let him see me here—don't let him take me back there."

The car passed slowly by only a short distance from her, the faint red splotches of its rear lights vanishing into the dense gray fog. Shivering partly with fear and partly because her dress was so wet with water that had dripped on her from the bushes, Annette waited cautiously where she was before daring to leave the protection of the hedge.

By this time Annette was convinced that Doan was looking for her and that it would be foolish to risk being seen on the street before she could get to Evelyn Summerall's house. Turning around and looking across the lawn behind her, Annette could see a faint light in somebody's house. It reminded her that Carl had told her to telephone for somebody to come for her and not to try to walk all the way to the other end of Flower Street. And now that Doan was probably driving up and down the street looking for her, she knew she should call Evelyn Summerall to come for her, and not risk being seen on the street by Doan.

Annette left the protection of the hedge and ran across the unlighted lawn as fast as she could toward the faint light she had seen at the house. In her haste, she stumbled in the darkness while trying to leap over a flowerbed and fell face downward on the lawn. When she got to her feet, she was relieved to find that she had not hurt herself and that her yellow dress was only slightly more wet and rumpled. Sweeping her damp hair away from her eyes and back over her shoulders, she made her way carefully to the front porch of the dwelling.

There was a small beam of light that made a bluish glow over the doorbell button, and she pushed it time and time again with a nervous urgency. She had no idea who lived in the sprawling high-roofed brick house, and she could not even think what it looked like in the daytime, although she knew she must have seen it from the street many times during the past several months since marrying Doan and coming to live in the same neighborhood.

There was no response to her ringing, and after a while she began pounding on the door with both hands.

She had just begun to wonder what she would do if nobody was at home when the door was cautiously opened a few inches and she had a glimpse of a portion of a scowling youthful face.

Relieved, she immediately leaned forward with a hopeful smile as she tried to see more of the face through the narrow opening.

"What the hell do you want?" a youthful voice demanded roughly from the other side of the door.

"I need to call somebody—please let me use your phone," she pleaded. "It's very important . . . an emergency. I'd appreciate it very much if you'll let me use the phone for just a minute."

The door was opened a little wider, and Annette could see a boy about fifteen or sixteen years old with long black hair falling over his ears and neck to his shoulders. The pale young face was thin, with a deeply fixed expression of defiance and hostility.

"You didn't tell me what I asked you." His voice was unpleasantly harsh and unfriendly, and he was staring at her with a sullen scowl. "Who the hell are you? What's your name?"

When she did not answer his questions immediately, he pointed at her dress from neck to hem.

"How did you get so wet like that?" he asked curiously. "Looks like you've been slopping around in a puddle somewhere."

"That doesn't matter," Annette said to him. "All I want is to use the phone. Please let me. It's a real emergency. Honest, it is! Will you?"

"Who do you want to phone to?"

"A friend."

"Why? What do you want to phone about?"

"I want somebody to come for me in a car."

"Your car break down?"

"No."

"No flat tire? Not out of gas?"

"No, nothing like that."

"Then why don't you call a taxi? Why do you want to bother your friends on a rough night like this?"

It was as if he were reminding her that Carl had advised her to call a taxicab to take her across town, but she was still fearful of what could happen if Doan saw her in a taxi. More than ever then, she felt that she would be safe only with Evelyn Summerall while crouching down on the floor of the car out of sight.

"What makes you keep on shaking your head like that for?" he asked her. "Why can't you phone for a cab like I said?"

"I'd rather call my friend."

The boy with the pale, thin face and long black hair turned away. Annette could hear him saying something to another person behind the door, but not distinctly enough to know what was being said.

Presently the boy appeared again at the doorway.

"Who's out there with you?" he demanded in a suspicious voice.

"Nobody," she told him.

"You really all by yourself?"

"Yes."

"I don't want any snooping going on around here, and I wouldn't like it if you lied to me."

"Honest, there's nobody else," she tried to tell him as convincingly as possible. "I'm all alone."

"And that's what it's all about? You just want to phone somebody to come get you?"

"Yes, and it is an emergency and I'm in such a hurry," she said impatiently, annoyed by the continued questioning and still not being permitted to use the phone. "Please let me—"

"Tell me something else. If your car didn't conk out, and if you're not out of gas and don't have a flat, what the hell kind of emergency are you talking about?"

"I told you that," she tried to reply as pleasantly as possible and hoping to be able to put an end to so much questioning. "All I want is to get somebody to come for me."

"Then it sounds to me like you've been walking out there on the street tonight and not driving a car. Is that so?"

"Yes."

"Why?"

Annette, refusing to answer the question, was so annoyed by that time that she was on the verge of leaving. She had taken a step backward when the door was opened wider and she could see the young boy standing there in full view. He was smiling at her for the first time then, and intimately appraising her from head to foot. A moment later he motioned to her to come back to where she had been standing at the door.

"I got something I want to tell you," he said.

"What is it?"

"Maybe you don't have to phone anybody for a while."

"I don't know what you mean," Annette said.

"How'd you like to find out?"

"But what is it—?"

The door was opened all the way, and instantly she was grasped by her arm and pulled into the hall. What was happening had begun so suddenly that she was too surprised to say anything when she found herself standing there in the dimly lighted hall and hearing the door slammed shut behind her and locked loudly.

"We've got something super going for us," the boy with the pale, thin face was saying. "Let's hurry up and get acquainted now that we're all here so we can get the party started. My name's Mike, and my fine towheaded friend here's name is Randy. That's us—Mike and Randy. Now, let's hear what to call you."

Annette was so frightened by what had been implied that she could only stare speechlessly at the two young boys. Seeing Mike and Randy, both big boys in tight jeans and unbuttoned shirts, in the hallway made her realize how uneasy she was to be here alone with them and how helpless she would be if they kept her there by force. Loud hard-rock music was coming from a stereo system in an adjoining room, and she could smell a funny kind of smoke that had a distinctly unusual odor that was not at all like cigarette or pipe tobacco.

(2)

"IT'S taking too much time for you to tell us what your name is," Mike complained. "What the hell is it?"

Annette said nothing.

"Why not?" Randy asked her then.

She still did not say anything.

"How about this?" Randy said with a pleasant smile. "If you don't want to tell us your real name, that's okay. But how about a substitute name? Betty? Susan? Gloria? Mildred?"

Mike was shaking his head disapprovingly. As he had been from the beginning, he remained glum and unsmiling as he watched Annette. She was becoming more afraid of Mike all the time, and fearing that there was no parent or other adult in the house to protect her, she glanced appealingly at Randy. When he looked at her then, it was startling to see how much he reminded her of Wayne, with his blue eyes and blond hair and the crinkling of his cheeks as he smiled.

"That's no good, Randy," Mike said with a deprecating wave of his hand. "None of those names look like her. We can think up something better for her. You know what I mean. Something suitable for the occasion."

"Like what?" Randy asked.

"Hell, I don't know. Let's all get acquainted now. That's the best way to find out what a good name for her will be. Let's go. Come on."

"Maybe we ought to let her go if she doesn't want to get acquainted, Mike."

"You bastard, you!" Mike said angrily. "When I saw her at the door to start with and asked you about it, you said you'd want to make it with her if I did. I haven't changed my mind. What the hell's wrong with you?"

Randy, glancing aside, could see Annette watching him with a tense look on her face.

"Okay, Mike. Who's going to make it with her first?"

"I'll be fair, Randy. We'll fist-fight about it."

"Wait a minute," Randy said. "Let's settle on a name for her before anything else. Since she has so much of that long brown hair and those big brown eyes and all that make her so pretty . . ."

"What about it?"

"Don't you see, Mike? Let's call her 'Brownie.' "

"You didn't think of that first," he said in his quarrelsome manner. "I was thinking of it before you did."

"You want to fist-fight about it?"

"Sure! I'll fist-fight you about both things at the same time. That'll show you who's boss around here."

Hunching their shoulders, they crouched forward and began jabbing harmlessly at each other with their fists. After they had pretended to be boxing for a while, Annette turned and ran as fast as she could to the front door. Just as she got to the door and before she was able to unlock it, both Mike and Randy sprang forward and grasped her arms.

"If I can't use the phone, then please let me go!" she pleaded with tears in her eyes. "This is so awful. You have no right to do this to me. If you'll let me go, I won't tell on you. I promise I won't do anything like that if only you'll let me go. Please!"

Randy turned to unlock the door for her and was pushing his way between Mike and Annette so she would have a chance to get away.

"What the hell do you think you're trying to do?" Mike demanded angrily. "Get away from that door and quit pushing me around. This is my house, and I saw her first, and she's staying here as long as I want her."

Roughly shoving Randy aside, and with a firm grip on her arm, Mike took Annette down the hall to the room where the hard-rock stereo music was so loud that it would have been useless to try to say anything until the sound was turned down to a much lower volume. After that, Mike still did not release his grip on her arm until he had taken her to one of the large couches and was sitting beside her.

The room where they were then was a richly decorated and expensively furnished informal parlor or library with deep-seated couches and lounge chairs and shaded reading lamps. There were bookcases and magazine stands and a chess table in the room, and at one side there was a complete bar with rows of bottles and glasses on the shelving. The heavy draperies and thick carpeting, as well as the upholstered chairs and couches, were in various shades of green.

Randy had followed Mike and Annette from the hall, and he went to a chair not far from the couch where they were sitting. With a cautious turning of her head, Annette could see Randy glancing at her with a look of concern on his face. She felt then that she would be protected as much as possible as long as he was in the same room with her, so as brief as it had to be to keep Mike from being antagonized, she smiled gratefully at Randy.

"Brownie," Mike said as he pointed at Randy, "I'll tell you a little about my pal over there—that handsome bastard with his blond hair and blue eyes. He's acting real funny tonight, and I don't know what excuses to make for him. You saw him try to open that front door so you could get away, and that's so unusual I don't know how to explain it. We've been pals for a long time and do all kinds of things together. Things like a little pot here and a little pot there and taking a few drops when we feel we need them and sharing friendly females now and then.

"Well, Randy lives a couple of blocks up the street from here, and we have a rally like this tonight every once in a while. His folks are too damn strict, and they don't even like for me to hang around his house. That's why we always rally here at my house. We hadn't gone for doing much tonight so far, except taking a few drops and some drags and turning up the stereo to the top of the roof. That's about all there is to say about Randy. And I'm not going to apologize for him anymore. Let him do that himself. And if you don't like what he says and want to make it with me and not with him, it won't hurt my feelings if you say so. I'll run him out of the house and make it with you just with my own self alone."

On the far side of the room near the bar, and faintly above the loud stereo music, the telephone was ringing continuously. With a sweeping motion of his hand, Mike imperiously pointed first at Randy and then at the phone. Randy went across the room to the phone and spoke a few words to somebody and then came back to his chair.

"The hospital again, Mike," Randy told him. "They still want your dad, like they need him to save somebody's life, and I told them he wasn't here and we didn't know where he was or when he'd be back."

"Right," Mike said. "The old bastard ought to have a little time off on his own. He works the skin off his ass all day long at that hospital, and he ought to have a chance to try to have a fucking-good time once in a while. Brownie, you're new here and you wouldn't know my old man is a doctor, would you? They say he's a damn good surgeon with a sharp knife, and I sort of like the old son-of-a-bitch, even if he is my dad."

Mike had leaned over and put his hand on Annette's leg, and she was not able to push him away.

"Look here, Brownie," he said as he moved closer to her on the couch. "How come your clothes are so wet? I didn't notice that till I started feeling you."

She shrank as far away from him as she could, while he moved his hands intimately over her body.

"You could catch a bad cold in that wet dress. It's a damn lucky thing for you that I'm a doctor's son and know what to do about it. That's me—Michael Mitchell III."

He motioned to Randy. "How about fixing Brownie a great big oversized martini with a lemon peel like my old man makes when he's jacking up for a fucking-good sex rally with his third wife. You know how. Right, Randy?"

As Randy moved to the bar, Mike turned to Annette. "Okay, Brownie," he said. "How about you and me taking off tonight? Wouldn't you like that? We'll split and leave old blondy Randy dandy behind, and to hell with him. What do you say, Brownie? Just you and me?"

Annette, her hands clenched tensely on her lap, was becoming more frightened all the time. Nevertheless, she shook her head determinedly. It was then that Randy left the bar and crossed the room carefully balancing a large martini. She took it gratefully.

As she gazed up at Randy's face, she wondered if he realized that she trusted him to protect her from any abuse by the doctor's son.

"Brownie, did I do a good job on the martini?" Randy asked her. "I'm sure I'll have to mix a few and try them on myself before I can qualify as a high-class bartender."

"Take a sip, and you'll find out how good you made it."

After drinking from the glass, Randy handed it back to her.

"That's enough of that!" Mike said in a voice that was like a shout. "You're acting like a couple of fucking love-birds. Now, stop making eyes at her, Randy, and go sit down in that chair where you belong. If you don't watch out, we'll still have that fist-fight, and I'd end up making it double with Brownie and you'd end up getting none of it. That'd make you feel sorry for yourself, wouldn't it?"

Mike reached over and put his hand on Annette's leg in the same intimate way he had done the first time.

"You've had your martini to warm you up, Brownie, so now take off that wet dress and we'll hang it up to dry. It's a lucky thing I'm a doctor's son. Who else could tell you how to keep from ending up dead from pneumonia? Randy wouldn't know that. So let's get that wet dress off like I said."

Annette, with a cry of protest, was trying to keep Mike from unfastening her dress.

"Leave her alone," Randy said as he reached forward and tried to jerk Mike's hands away from Annette. "Don't do that to her, Mike. I don't want you to."

"Who the hell do you think you are?" Mike shouted. "You can't come in my house and try to tell me what I can't do! Get your hands off me and leave me alone!"

Jumping to his feet, Mike shoved Randy backward across the room. Then, with a quick movement he turned around and faced Annette.

"It won't do you any good to listen to him—you do what I tell you. And if you don't get that dress off in a hurry, I'll rip it off you."

Annette, her hands shaking, began unfastening the damp yellow dress.

"Please don't tear my dress," she begged. "You won't do that, will you?"

"Okay, but let's see you get into action."

While Annette was standing up and nervously removing her dress, Randy came back and grabbed Mike's arm.

"Stop making her do that if she doesn't want to," he told Mike. "You shouldn't do this to her—she's a stranger, and you know plenty of others—"

"Shut up, goddamn you!" he shouted. "I do as I please around here. And if you don't like it, get the hell out."

Annette had taken off her dress and was standing there clothed only in pink bikini panties and a scanty brassiere. She had been trembling with fear ever since Mike had threatened to rip her dress from her if she refused to obey him. Glancing from one boy to the other, she was still hopeful that Randy would be able to keep Mike from forcing her to submit to him as he had threatened to do. She was not surprised then when she realized she was hoping that Randy would be the one to have her sexually instead of Mike.

But it was Mike who reached up and pulled her down beside him on the couch. Sitting there while he hugged her with one arm around her neck and stroked her leg with his other hand, she wondered why she was making no effort to keep him from fondling her so intimately.

She no longer felt the need to worry about anything, only to enjoy the delightful warmth that crept through her body now that her damp dress had been removed.

Presently, from the far side of the room near the bar, and faintly above the sound of the stereo music, the telephone began ringing once more. After going across the room and speaking a few words to somebody on the phone, Randy came back to his chair.

"The hospital won't give up," he said to Mike. "They say it's an emergency, and they need him right away. I told them again he wasn't here and we didn't know where he was or when he'd be back. That was right, wasn't it?"

"Right," Mike said. He was holding Annette close to his chest and stroking her flowing brown hair. "The poor bastard, just married to his third wife, he ought to have more time to himself and not have to zip up his pants every time the phone rings from the hospital. He's a great guy, but I haven't got her figured out yet. I don't know what she'd do to me in a dark room with the door locked. If she comes along and puts it up, I'm going to give it to her straight and tell her that I'm not moving in on my old man's third wife. My dad's a real great bastard of a guy, and I sure wouldn't hustle his third wife for nothing you can think of. I'm a slimy son-of-a-bitch most of the time, but I've got a few good principles to live by, and that's one of them. You admire me for that, don't you, Randy, old pal?"

"I sure do, Mike," Randy replied. "You just keep on like you're going, and maybe soon you'll pick up some more good principles you can use."

"You dirty bastard! I know what you mean by that. You're trying to bullshit me out of having a fucking-good party with Brownie. What the hell happened to you? When she got here awhile ago, and you had your first look at her at the front door, you'd have jumped her right there and then if I hadn't cooled you down so we could get acquainted like we're doing now, to make the party a lot more friendly later. Now you're behaving like you're lovesick or something for her and don't want me to have my turn with her. What the hell? You think you can get rid of me and have her all for yourself?"

"It's nothing like that, Mike," Randy pleaded earnestly. "Let's let her go."

Mike laughed at him.

"If you make her stay here, Mike," Randy told him, "I'm not going to have anything to do with it."

"It's so damn good of you to give me exclusive rights, Randy! How can I ever thank you enough? I feel high on drops, but you must be a hell of a lot higher than I am to hand over your half-share of Brownie to me just because we're good schoolboy pals. It touches me in a real soft spot somewhere to know I've got an unselfish pal like you, Randy. I hope you can find yourself a fucking-good time if you can jack up a hard for it. And now that I've given thanks . . ."

Randy had left his chair and was standing uncertainly in the middle of the room while waiting to see if Mike was going to try to force Annette down on the couch, when there was a noisy clamor at the front of the house. First the doorbell was ringing, and then somebody was knocking loudly on the door.

Mike, after getting up from the couch, turned and glanced first at Annette and then at Randy.

"That might be somebody looking for her," he said with a worried frown on his pale face.

All three of them listened intently while the knocking on the front door became louder and sounded more insistent.

Mike was the first to speak after that. "Who'd be coming here looking for you?" he demanded suspiciously, glaring at Annette. "Who knows where you are?"

Annette was shaking her head. "I don't know—I don't!"

"If you lie to me, Brownie, you're going to be sorry."

"It's the truth—I really don't know."

Mike was walking toward Randy.

"She could've been planted here on us, Randy. She could be on the narc squad—a lady cop—they've been trying to get some pushers lately, and she could be after me, and more cops are trying to get in on a raid. But all I do is sell a few signed blank prescriptions when I swipe them from my old man's desk. They can't get me for that, can they, Randy?"

Mike was so frightened that his hands were trembling, and his thin face was so pale that it looked almost lifeless.

"I don't know about that, Mike," Randy said, "but you'd better find out who it is and then try to talk your way out of it."

"Okay," he said nervously. "While I'm going to the front door, you put Brownie in that storeroom behind the bar and keep her there out of sight. Whoever's trying to get in here would make bad trouble for us if they saw her like she is now. And when you get her in the storeroom, don't let her yell out or kick the door or anything like that. Do anything you have to do to keep her quiet, Randy."

At the last moment before hurrying to the front door, seeing Annette's yellow dress folded over the back of the chair where it had been placed for drying, Mike snatched it up and tossed it to Randy.

"Make her put that on to cover up—just in case," Mike told him. "And don't let her out of that storeroom, either."

After going into the small room behind the bar, Annette immediately put on her dress. Standing closely together in the narrow space, she and Randy waited tensely in the darkness of the windowless room while trying to hear what might be happening at the front of the house.

Presently Annette reached out for Randy, as if she had been a small child afraid of the dark. Feeling the trembling of her hand, he moved so close to her then that he could smell the fragrant perfume of hair and touch the yielding softness of her body.

So much had already taken place since leaving home that rainy evening; fearful of what else might happen to her before the night was over, Annette wished somebody would deliver her from her confused and tormented state of mind. In the darkness of the small room, she was beginning to wonder if she had been wise to let Evelyn rule her life with the casting of horoscopes and if she had made a mistake by not waiting a little longer and finding somebody of her own choice to marry. Confusingly pleasant yet disturbing thoughts were continually reminding her that

Randy, unlike Doan, was so very much like Wayne in appearance and personality that she wished she had known him before hastily consenting to marry Doan.

As if he knew what thoughts were in her mind, Randy put his arm around Annette, and almost instantly she pressed her face against his shoulder. She realized then how strongly she was attracted to him, even though she was almost twice his age.

"Do you have a sweetheart?" she asked in a whisper.

"No," Randy answered. "Nobody like that yet."

"I envy the girl you'll fall in love with and marry."

"You do? It's nice here with you, and I wish . . ."

"What, Randy?"

"I wish I knew your name. I know it's not really Brownie. It has to be something else."

"I'm Annette," she was quick to whisper to him.

"I'll stop Mike so you can get away. But where do you live? How can I find you?"

"Look in the phone book for the Jack Summerall address. That's where I'm going. And I'll be waiting . . ."

Annette could feel a delightful sensation in her body while Randy held her roughly and yet so lovingly in his arms, and she gradually moved her head on his shoulder until she could kiss the buttons on his shirt. While wondering how soon he would begin making love to her if they had not been confined in such a narrow space, she felt that she was being overcome with a feverish delirium.

It was at that moment that there was a sudden commotion in the hallway, with the loud slamming of the front door and the shrill sound of a woman's excited voice that could be heard distinctly inside the storeroom.

"I know who it is," Randy whispered to Annette. "Don't worry, it's nobody looking for you."

"But who is she?" Annette asked.

"That's Judy's mother. Judy's the fourteen-year-old girl

Mike's been playing around with. I've heard her before when she was looking for Judy. She always blames Mike when she can't find her."

Judy's mother had come into the living room from the hall by that time, and her voice was loud enough to be heard anywhere in the house.

"Where is she?" she demanded.

"I don't know," Mike said. "Don't ask me."

"You don't know!" she said excitedly. "I wouldn't trust you for one second. Even if you told me a hundred times you don't know where Judy is now, I still wouldn't believe you. I know you too well by now. Are you hiding her somewhere in this house? Have you seen her tonight? Where is she?

"Maybe she's hiding from you at home."

"She most certainly is not. She told me she was going to turn out the light in her room and go to sleep early tonight, and when I looked in her room a little while ago, she wasn't there. Like she's done before, she crawled out the window and went somewhere. Where did she go?"

"Don't blame me," Mike said. "I don't look after Judy. That's your business."

"Please help me, Michael," she begged. "I don't want anything bad to happen to Judy. She's only fourteen. I've got to do everything I can to protect her."

"I'm not sure, but I heard there was going to be a late party for window-crawlers tonight."

"Where?" she pleaded. "Please tell me!"

"A couple of blocks down the street."

"But where? At what address?"

"That's all I know about it."

"I just don't trust you," she said doubtfully. "She could be hiding in a closet right this minute. I know she's been over here many times lately."

"Take your choice—look for her here or somewhere else. It's all the same to me."

"Where are your parents tonight, Michael? Are you here all alone?"

"You can see for yourself, can't you?"

"There are some things I wish I couldn't see."

"Then shut your eyes and go away."

Nothing more was said, and the only sound to be heard was the closing of the front door as Judy's mother left the house. Moments later the storeroom door was flung open, and Mike was looking at Annette and Randy as they stood there with their arms around each other.

"What the hell!" he shouted at them. "That's being too damn cozy. You wanted to call a taxi and let her go? Is that what you've still got in mind, Randy?"

"That's right, Mike. Let's let her go."

"You bastard!" Mike shouted at him. "I'll show you!"

Turning around, Mike reached for the sharp-pointed knife on the bar that was used for peeling lemons to make twists for drinks. Just as Mike grabbed the knife, Randy got to him in time to knock it from his grasp, and it was sent hurling all the way across the room and fell on the floor after striking the wall. By then Randy was able to lock his arm around Mike's neck with a viselike stranglehold.

"Hurry and phone for somebody to come for you," Randy told Annette. "I can hold him while you're calling."

"I don't know where I am," she said urgently. "What is this address?"

"Twelve-twenty Flower Street."

Mike was struggling to free himself, but he was still helpless with the strangling hold Randy had around his neck.

"You bastard," he muttered weakly. "I'll get you for this . . . Randy . . . you bastard."

After Annette had nervously dialed Evelyn's number, the phone rang several times and finally was answered by Jack Summerall.

"I want to speak to Evelyn," she said hurriedly.

"Evelyn's not here now," Jack told her, "but you sound like somebody I know."

"I'm Annette . . . I'm calling Evelyn . . . I want to ask her to come for me. It's important."

"What's the trouble, Annette?" Jack asked.

"I can't tell you now . . . later . . . but if Evelyn . . ."

"She went visiting. It's sort of her night out with the girls. She won't be back for two or three hours."

"But I can't wait!"

"I'll come for you, Annette. Where are you now?"

"It's twelve-twenty Flower Street."

"Who lives there?"

"I don't know . . . I'm not sure, but I told you the street address. And I'll be in front of the house waiting for you."

"All right, Annette. Don't worry anymore. I'm on my way already."

As Annette was running across the room from the telephone to the hallway, she wanted to stop and kiss Randy to let him know how grateful she was for what he was doing for her. She did not stop, though. Mike might grab her if she went that close, and then free himself from Randy's choking hold around his neck.

Reaching the doorway to the hall, she did stop to look back at Randy. That was when she saw the shiny sharp-pointed bar knife on the floor. She hastily picked it up and took it with her so Mike would not be able to get his hands on it and use it to free himself from Randy.

Part SIX

AS soon as she had left the large two-story house, Annette began thinking how fortunate she was to have escaped. Until then she had been too frightened to realize how close she had come to being forced to strip completely naked and compelled to perform and satisfy Mike sexually in whatever way he demanded.

Even though Annette was safely out of the house, she was sorry not to have had a chance to let Randy know in some way, other than the quick smile she gave him as she was hurrying from the room, how grateful she was for his help. If it had not been for Randy and his sympathy for her, she surely would be a captive of the doctor's son at this very moment.

She could still remember the excitement she felt at the caressing touch of Randy's hands while she was being pressed so intimately to his body in the narrow storeroom. As she let herself think about Randy without restraint, it was to her like actually experiencing the thrill and ecstasy of his lovemaking.

"Randy, you're so very dear to me," Annette whispered. "I wish there could be a way for us to be alone together again. I don't know what's going to happen to me now. But I'll need somebody, and I wish you were here."

In her haste to escape from Mike and reach the street, Annette had almost lost her footing several times as she hurried down the path in the dim light. Even though there was nobody within sight and no sound of footsteps behind her, she could not keep from being frightened in the night.

When she finally reached the sidewalk at Flower Street, she stood there for a minute trying to control her nervousness. Presently she looked down and saw that she was still clutching the sharp-pointed bar knife she had carried away with her.

Her first thought was to put it into her purse in case she needed something to protect herself. Her next thought, however, was that she would have no need for such a dangerous object, because Jack Summerall had promised to come for her, and as soon as he got here, she would be safe.

The more she thought about it, and looking at the flickering gleam of light on the long shiny blade of the bar knife, Annette knew she would be too afraid to keep it even out of sight in her purse when it was a weapon that could be taken from her by force by somebody and used to stab her to death. She had no fear that Jack Summerall would do such a thing, but nevertheless, without waiting another moment, she hurled the knife as far away as she could in the direction of the dark hedgerow between the sidewalk and the house she had left a few minutes before.

As she walked nervously back and forth while waiting for Jack to get there, Annette tried to keep from thinking how frightened she was by talking aloud to herself.

"He'll be here any second now," she was whispering bravely. "He said he'd come right away, and there's no reason why he wouldn't be telling the truth. It's a very short distance for him to drive, and nothing could happen to keep him from getting here. And he certainly knew I needed him to come for me. It wouldn't be like Evelyn or her husband not to keep a promise—well, it wouldn't be like Evelyn, but I really don't know enough about Jack to be certain. But Jack knew how urgent it was—he could tell that by the way I talked on the phone; he'll come for me, he'll get here any second now."

As the minutes passed and Jack Summerall still did not come, Annette had the terrifying thought that he might have forgotten or misunderstood the address she had given him over the phone.

Just then an automobile with headlights beaming brightly nearly a block away came down Flower Street directly toward her. Leaning over the curb, Annette waved frantically so she would be seen at once.

"Jack! Here I am!" she called loudly, long before she could see anybody in the automobile.

With a screeching of tires on the pavement and a sudden lurching of the car, the driver slowed down as soon as he saw Annette waving frantically with both hands. However, even though the driver had slowed down, he did not stop at the curb.

No longer blinded by the bright headlights then, but before she could see the color of the automobile, she suddenly had the terrifying thought that Doan might still be driving through the streets in search of her. She knew that Doan could get out of his car and easily catch her before she could run off and hide from him in the darkness. Fearful of what could happen, Annette held her breath while trying to see if the car had the familiar color of Doan's dark green sedan.

As the car passed slowly only a few feet from where she stood at the curb, Annette recognized the strange man who had spoken to her earlier that evening and tried to persuade her to get into his paint-faded brown sedan. Even though she had had only a fleeting glimpse of the man in the noisy old automobile, she had been quick to realize that it was her fault for waving to him before she knew who he was, and she hoped that he had not recognized her.

Watching the car go out of sight around the next corner, Annette was relieved that the car had not stopped at the curb and that the man with the disturbing way of staring at her had not tried a second time to get her into the car with him.

Even though the old faded sedan was no longer to be seen, she wondered what she would do if the driver went around the block and came back again. Now that she had seen the strange man twice that night, she knew she would never be able to forget his balding head, with a thin fringe of hair above his ears, and his heavy-jowled face.

All she could do now was wait to find out if the man in the bright blue shirt would drive around the block and then come back, or if he would leave the neighborhood. This was the moment when she had to decide whether to hide from him or stay where she was with the expectation that Jack Summerall would get there in time to take her safely away.

Listening intently for the faintest sound of an automobile coming from any direction, she began to wonder if it would have been wise to keep the daggerlike bar knife she had brought from the doctor's house, instead of hurling it off into the darkness. She tried to decide whether she would be able to find the knife if she went looking for it at the hedge.

It did not take her long, though, with her memory of the man in the brown sedan, to decide that the knife could easily be taken from her. After that, even if she screamed at the top of her voice, she could be forced into the car and taken to some secluded place before Randy or anybody else could get there to help her.

Becoming more frightened by the minute, and uncertain what to do, she suddenly saw the headlights of a car appear less than a block away. Instead of moving slowly, this time the automobile was speeding rapidly toward her down Flower Street. She closed her eyes prayerfully, with the fervent hope that the driver, if not Jack Summerall or Carl in the police patrol car, would be Doan and not the man in the blue shirt she feared so much.

A few seconds later, the car came to a tire-squeaking stop at the curb.

THE door to the front seat sprang open for her.

"You look exactly like the person I think you are, but if I didn't know your name, I'd still think you're the most charming pickup on the street tonight." Jack spoke in his usual breezy manner, but he was looking at her questioningly. "What goes? You phoned me like the house was on fire, to begin with, and now I find you standing here on the street all alone at this time of night."

Jack reached for Annette and drew her close to him. The door was closed and the engine was still running, but he made no move to drive away.

"I would've been here sooner," he explained, "but I thought it would be smart to stop at a filling station. I knew you wouldn't have much of an opinion of a guy who took you for a ride in his car and ran out of gas."

"I'm so glad you came for me, Jack," she said earnestly, "it doesn't matter now how long it took you to get here. The important thing is you're here. I don't know what would've happened to me if you hadn't come. It's been terrible. Part of the time I didn't know what was real and what was unreal—that's how confused I was. I thought I could hear voices, and I was talking too, but I'm so confused, I don't know what to think even now."

"Well, I'm very much real," he told her.

"I know you are, and I'm so grateful, and I want to thank you over and over for coming to get me."

With a sudden movement, Annette leaned over and kissed Jack several times.

After that, instead of leaving, Jack switched off the headlights and stopped the engine.

"Why did you do that?" Annette asked in surprise, glancing first at Jack and then looking across the dark lawn toward the doctor's house. "Why don't we leave? We don't have to stay here any longer, do we?"

"There're two reasons, Annette. One is that your sexy kisses put notions in my mind, and the other is that I'm just plain curious. The notions will keep till they're ready to be put to use, but right now I want to know what this is all about. I would say something very unusual has been taking place tonight. Now, tell me straight, Annette. What happened? Have you been raped?"

She was quick to shake her head. "No. Not that."

"Well, if you say so, but if you want to know what I think, I'd say your pretty yellow dress looks wrinkled and damp, like you've been out in the rain for several hours, and you have a sort of hungry look that a person would have after missing dinner tonight. How about some explaining? And if you don't tell me all about it, I'll have to start trying to guess what happened, and that means there'll be no limit to what I'll think of. Is that too much to ask of you, Annette?"

She smiled slightly. "I suppose not."

Sitting there in the car with Jack and feeling so safe and protected after what had taken place during the past several hours, all she wanted to do was cry and cry. As she began sobbing, Jack took a handkerchief from his pocket and gave it to her. He patted her hand comfortingly until she was no longer crying.

"Just between us—me and you—tell me what happened, Annette. Did Doan Thurmond turn out to be such a mean old son-of-a-bitch that you ran away from him? Is that it?"

"Why would you think that?" she replied evasively.

"I only know as much as Evelyn wants to tell me."

"What did she tell you?"

"Not enough to make much of a scandal. All I heard was that you wanted a baby and he didn't. If that's true, then I'd guess you'd gotten so uptight from being denied motherhood that you were ready to leave home and look for somebody who would gladly accommodate you. That's my personal guess, so don't blame Evelyn for what I said. Evelyn's got enough to jump on me about, and I can't afford to let her have something else to find fault about."

"I don't want to make any trouble for you, Jack," she told him earnestly. "Don't worry. Let's just not talk about that anymore."

There was a long interval of silence, and then Annette suddenly turned to Jack and put both arms around his neck and hugged him desperately. She had never been so intimate with him during all the time she had known Evelyn and had visited them in their home, and she was surprised that she was doing such a thing at that moment. As she thought about what she was doing, though, she knew it was because she had a compelling urge to express gratitude for his sympathy and because he had come to protect her from the danger of being alone on the street. With a final tightening of her arms around his neck, she kissed him fervently several times.

"I'm so grateful, Jack," she said, moving away. "I don't know what would've happened to me—something terrible!"

"I didn't know I deserved all that hugging and kissing,

but I sure do know how to appreciate it, and it's something to remember." He moved closer to her and stroked her long brown hair with caressing touches. "Now, if I could think of something else to remember you by . . ."

"Can't we go now, Jack?" she spoke up uneasily.

"While we're still here at the scene of some of your night's activity, I want you to tell me what's been going on. Is it anything you're afraid to tell me about? Ashamed of?"

"No, Jack. But I don't want to stay here any longer. Please take me to Evelyn."

"Don't be in such a rush," he told her harshly. "I want to know what happened here to make you so jumpy and in such a hurry to get away now."

"I wish you wouldn't make me—"

"I'm asking, not making."

"Well, what do you want me to tell you?"

"Tell me about that house you phoned from. Who lives there?"

"A doctor."

"What's his name?"

"I don't know," Annette said.

"Then how do you know he's a doctor?"

"Somebody there told me."

"You mean you went to that house and said you wanted to use the telephone to call me—"

"To call Evelyn," Annette reminded him.

"All right. To call Evelyn. And you went to a strange house to do that? All alone at this time of night?"

"Yes, but—"

"Yes! But! You haven't told me anything yet. What's this all about? You wouldn't leave home and go to a doctor's house and not know what his name is and phone for me to come get you, unless something mighty strange is going on, and that's what I'm asking you about. Now, what are you going to say?"

"Please, Jack," she begged. "I'm so nervous being here. Let's leave. I don't want to stay here any longer."

"All right, Annette," he said agreeably, smiling and reaching over and putting his hand on her leg. "Don't you worry. We'll go now. And the way I see it, you look more hungry than anything else. That could be your big trouble. Leaving home in a hurry before you had dinner. But it's not too late for dinner, and I know a good restaurant where we can go to and—"

With both of her hands, Annette tried to move Jack's hand from her leg, and at the same time she was shaking her head in a gesture of distress.

"What's the matter?" he asked.

"My dress—just look at it. It's so rumpled and awful-looking." Reaching over his hand, she tried to smooth the skirt over her legs, but the wrinkles in the yellow cloth would not disappear. "I'd be so embarrassed to be seen looking like this in public, Jack. I'd be so conspicuous. Please don't take me where I'd be embar.assed like that— I'd rather starve."

"You don't have to worry or starve," he told her reassuringly. "We'll go to a drive-in spot not far from here where we can sit in the car and get you their best roast-beef sandwich or biggest hamburger and all the chocolate ice cream and chocolate layer cake you want. Doesn't that sound good to you, Annette? Then, after that you can lean back and relax and tell me all about this mysterious night on the town you've got going for yourself. How about that?"

"I am hungry, Jack, and I would like to have something to eat. But Evelyn—she's not with us. So I think we ought to go straight to your house right now, and I'll ask Evelyn to make me a sandwich—any kind will do. And that'll be enough for me. I shouldn't be going somewhere in public like this—I mean, with you at night. . . ."

"Why not? You phoned for me to come get you."

"Yes, but when I called, I thought Evelyn would be at home and she'd come for me. I had no idea you'd come."

"Well, what's so bad about that?"

"The thing about it—the way it is—it's like having a date with you and I shouldn't . . ."

"Annette, it's exactly like I said on the phone," he said with an intimate lowering of his voice. "Evelyn is not at home now, and it'll be a lot later than this when she does come back. She went to somebody's house on the north side of Zephyrfield where they're having one of their club meetings tonight. It's probably the monthly meeting of the FFF—the Female Freedom Franchise—and you know yourself how the girls like to stay up late and eat ginger cookies and drink a lot of red wine and gossip to all hours when they get together like that. So that's the way it is. Now, do you want to get out of this car and wait here on the street by yourself half the night till Evelyn can come for you? Or are you going to be sensible and stay in the car with me?"

"Don't go away and leave me here on the street all alone, Jack. Everything is so dark and scary." A shiver passed through her body, and she moved closer to him. "But being like this—with you—when Evelyn is somewhere else . . ."

"I know what you mean, Annette. You keep on thinking it's like having a date. And if you want to know how I feel about it, I can't think of anything nicer than having a cozy wrap-around date with you tonight. And if you want to know something else, I've often thought about what it would be like to have a horizontal night with you. I've always liked your sexy looks, and I've wondered a lot of times how you'd treat a man where the treating feels best. But I'll tell you more about it when we get you something to eat. Now we're going to be off and running!"

Annette was clinging to his arm with both of her hands then. He had started the engine, but the automobile had not moved.

"But, Jack," she said presently, "what will Evelyn think, when she knows . . . ?"

"There'll be nothing for her to think about if she never knows anything."

"But Evelyn and I are such true friends—we always tell each other everything."

"Everything? Suppose we left here now and went to a motel and checked into a room for the rest of the night— would you tell her about it?"

"Jack! You know I'd never do that!"

"Well, I don't know for sure that you wouldn't, but I wouldn't consider it a waste of time trying to find out before the night's over."

The big yellow sports car was thrust into motion with a resounding roar and a jolting surge of power that sent it speeding down Flower Street with its bright headlights leading the way.

"Jack, where are you taking me now?" Annette called to him, raising her voice above the sound that the car was making. "I could never go to a motel with you. Never! Jack, I do trust you. But please tell me where we're going."

"You couldn't forget that," he answered lightly. "You remember. We're going to get you something to eat."

"And you won't make me go to another place with you —to a motel or hotel?"

"Would it make you feel better if I promised not to make you do that?"

"Yes, I'd feel much better."

"Then it's a promise. No motel room tonight."

Without another word spoken, Annette reached up and kissed his cheek several times.

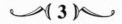

CAREFULLY avoiding Jack's glances at her as they went toward Eastern Boulevard, and thinking about how he stroked her legs and his remarks about a motel room, Annette wondered if he had been intentionally trying to deceive her when he said Evelyn would not be at home until much later that night. More than ever, then, she could not keep from being suspicious and mistrustful, even though he had promised not to make her go to a motel, and she hoped she would not have to be alone with him much longer that night.

Having known Evelyn and Jack Summerall ever since she and Wayne came to Zephyrfield and she began teaching a kindergarten class at the public school, which was long before Wayne's tragic death and her grief of widowhood, Annette had felt from the beginning that she was exceedingly fortunate to have such a close and trustworthy friend as Evelyn.

It was due to their friendship that several times recently Evelyn had confided to Annette how hurt she was to know about the way Jack frequently ran around with other women in Zephyrfield and to have the town gossip constantly relayed to her.

"Annette," Evelyn had said during one of the times when they were talking confidentially, "Annette, I can't help it. I've come to suspect every female in this town between the ages of eight and eighty—with the exception of you, thank

God! I'm so desperately suspicious that I can't even look at another woman without hating her for being female, because I have this agonizing feeling that she's probably already been to bed with Jack or will be going to bed with him soon. But not you, Annette. Never. I know you too well. I trust you. I could never doubt your loyalty and friendship."

"Of course, Evelyn," she had been quick to say. "You'll never have to worry about me—about that."

"I know you're sincere, and I believe you, Annette. But there's something I want you to remember, and this is important. Don't ever let Jack fool you—be careful when you're with him—don't let him persuade you to do something that would allow him to take advantage of you. I know he'd like to get you to go to bed with him—I know that for sure. There are many signs that I've learned to interpret expertly. So please be careful, Annette. Don't trust him. *Never* trust him, no matter how nicely he treats you."

Evelyn had told Annette that there had been many times during the past several years when she was on the verge of leaving Jack and taking their young children with her. Whenever this had occurred, Evelyn said that inevitably something always reminded her of the joy and bliss of their love at the time of their marriage. It was at that moment that she began crying her heart out that she had always changed her mind and decided to give Jack one more chance, while he in turn tearfully promised to stop his humiliating behavior for her sake.

Nevertheless, Evelyn had said there was a limit to the number of times she could accept his worthless promises and be persuaded not to leave him. This was when she had told Annette not to be surprised if suddenly she made up her mind to get a divorce as quickly as possible before Jack could talk her out of it.

"I've tried and tried to do everything I can imagine a

woman could do to please Jack and make him want to stay with me and not go off the way he does. I still love him very much, and maybe I always will, no matter how awfully he treats me. I can't help it—even though I don't know where he is and when he'll come home. I want to be so loving to him, but he's not here."

"I'm so sorry, Evelyn," Annette would say sympathetically.

On such occasions Evelyn would become so upset that she would begin sobbing brokenly and be able to talk no further about her unhappiness.

Thinking of Evelyn and her unhappiness, Annette glanced wonderingly at Jack and tried to assure herself that she was safe in his company and would soon be taken to Evelyn at the Summerall home. She had been so tense and uneasy for such a long time that she could not keep from leaning backward with a weary sigh and closing her eyes peacefully for a few moments.

("I don't mind telling you what I think Jack Summerall's trouble is. And don't forget that I like Jack, although there are those who call him a frigging bastard and a wife-cheating S.O.B. I buy my insurance from his wife's agency, and we're good poker-playing friends, and I'll say anything to his face that I'd say behind his back. Well, the main trouble with Jack is that he came along in a generation that was fed so much sugar and cream by indulgent parents that he still wants everything in life to be either a candy bar or an ice-cream cone.

("Then along came a wonderful girl named Evelyn who had just inherited a family insurance business, and Jack was quick to foresee a life of ease for himself. They married, which is proper for a woman of almost any age, and which can be the best deal a man can make in life if he's ready for it, but for which Jack was in no way qualified except that he was of legal age to apply for a marriage license. What I'm saying is that Jack wanted to marry rich, and he did, and he wants to continue acquiring sexual partners, and he does.

("As my wife says about Jack, you never know in advance who the next woman is who'll be given the heartbreaking treat-and-mistreat deal, and all you can do is feel sorry for her when it's all over and too late for a friendly warning. And I agree with my wife when she says that a wonderful person like Evelyn Summerall doesn't deserve to have to suffer continually knowing Jack is out there somewhere with another woman.")

After the passing of the rain and the fog and the dismal hours earlier in the evening, the weather was clear and pleasant shortly before midnight when Annette and Jack got to the Tic-Toc Drive-Inn in the midst of the nightlife activity along the colorful neon-lighted strip on Eastern Boulevard.

As usual at that time of night, there were no vacant parking spaces left in front of the popular night spot, and Jack had to go to the far side of the parking lot, where he found one of the few spaces left. The lighting was dim in the secluded corner, and at that distance the sound of the hard-rock music over the loudspeaker was not too loud for conversation.

Jack switched off the engine, lit a cigarette, and leaned back in his seat.

"I was real worried there for a minute," he said in an easy manner as he reached for her and drew her closer. "I was afraid there'd be no place for us here at the Tic-Toc, but the way it turned out, we've got the best parking spot in the whole lot. How do you like our luck so far, Annette? Makes everything nice and cozy, huh?"

"Jack," she began nervously, "I don't know what to say, but I wish . . ."

"I know what to say, Annette. Here we are in our private little corner of the world where we can snuggle up close and be cozy all by ourselves. Now, nobody can bother us

while you're telling me why a beautiful young lady like
you left home on a rotten rainy night and what you were
doing at a doctor's house whose name you said you don't
even know and calling me on the phone to come get you
in a hurry. Now, go ahead and tell me what this mystery is
all about."

Annette felt a nervous tenseness come over her as she
was reminded how much she had been frightened by the
man in the blue shirt and by the drug-induced behavior of
the doctor's son.

"All I wanted to do was see Evelyn tonight," she told
him. "I didn't know there'd be so much trouble. And that's
still all I want to do—Evelyn will help me."

"That doesn't explain anything to me. Your trouble now
is that you're hungry. You're so hungry that it's making
you shake all over. You're going to be getting all you want
to eat, and that'll make you feel better, and then you can
tell me everything. A car-hop girl ought to get here to take
our order any minute now. All we have to do is be patient
and wait for our turn, because this place is really jumping
with people who got here ahead of us. Now, just relax and
remember that I'm going to take good care of you."

Annette, moving restlessly on the seat beside him, had
turned and was looking pleadingly at Jack.

"All I want is for you to take me to Evelyn. Please do
that right away. She must be there by now—it's after midnight. I don't have to stay here for something to eat—I'm
not hungry now. Will you do that for me, Jack? Please!"

"No," he said emphatically, "because there's something
I'm going to tell you, and there's so much of it that it will
probably take all night long. What I'm going to tell you
starts out about you and me and Doan Thurmond."

"What do you mean? How could that concern you?"

"Don't you want to wait for something to eat first?"

"No. I want to know what you're talking about."

"All right, Annette," he said calmly, "and I'll be giving

it to you straight, so there won't be any misunderstanding. You are beautiful. There's nobody else like you. You have the kind of sexy look about you that would get any man down on his knees for you. I've wanted you ever since the first time I saw you, and after waiting all this time, I'm not going to quit till I get you. And when I say I want you, I mean right down the middle, and you know where that is. Do you understand my language, Annette? Is it plain enough?"

Instead of speaking, she put her hand over her mouth and nodded with a slight motion of her head.

"That's good," he said. "I'm glad I'm getting to you. And now I can tell you what's been bothering me. When Doan Thurmond saw you at that cocktail party at our house and asked you on the spot to marry him . . . well, I wanted to shoot him dead right there and then. And how I wish I had! Anyway, after you did marry him, making the excuse that it was because Wayne had said he wanted somebody to take care of you, that was when I spent a lot of time hoping something would happen that would make you leave Doan Thurmond. And now the best thing I ever wished for has come true. You left him. And now I've got you, and I'm going to have you the way I want you."

"But, Jack, what I've done tonight has nothing to do with you."

"Well, no matter what, I know one thing for sure. I'm at the right place at the right time. And now, while we're waiting for you to get something to eat, I want you to take off those dangerous sharp-edged earrings and put them away. I'm going to be whispering something personal in your ear, and I don't want to be battle-scarred when I get that close to you."

Part SEVEN

CHERRY Creek Park, which in earlier times had been a part of the large estate of a wealthy pioneer family before being donated to the city of Zephyrfield for public use, was an extensive area of ponds and groves and botanical gardens several miles beyond Eastern Boulevard's boisterous night-life strip of bars and cafés and go-go joints.

Zephyrfield's only public park, and a magnificent showplace of year-round greenery, it was situated a considerable distance from the nearest residential district, and fortunately, also, was far enough away from the grinding turmoil of highways to be able to offer all citizens a quiet and tranquil place of rest and recreation day and night.

As many people in Zephyrfield said, they were not only proud of the natural beauty of the park itself, but also they could take pride in the fact that year after year police records revealed that a person was more likely to be mugged or assaulted or otherwise molested in downtown Zephyrfield than in Cherry Creek Park.

The driveways and parking lots were patrolled from time to time both day and night, but even then the police did not linger very long, and only rarely did they get out of their patrol cars while they were in the park and annoy anybody with lengthy questionings and identity checks.

For the most part, the people who made a habit of frequently visiting the park during daylight hours were local family picnickers and youthful sunbathers and peaceable bird-watchers. On moonlight nights, and particularly in the warm months of spring and summer, there were usually numerous couples—both white and black—to be seen seated on the benches and strolling along the paths. In cool weather, a few of the younger couples sometimes left their automobiles and rolled up in blankets on the lawns.

In addition to the usual playground equipment and conveniences provided for visitors of all ages, including sandboxes and seesaws and merry-go-rounds and shuffleboard courts and inexpensive snack bars, among the most popular attractions were two sizable ponds that had been formed by impounding water from Cherry Creek. One of these was a large freshwater duck pond located on the north side of the park, and the other one was a lily pond, equally as large, on the south side. Canoes and flat-bottom rowboats were available for rent to those who wanted to paddle on a pond and feed the ducks or merely to drift lazily among the lily pads.

For the convenience of visitors who came in private automobiles to stay for only an hour or to spend the whole day, and for out-of-towners arriving in buses on garden-club tours, the city provided ample parking spaces without meters or restrictions on all the streets surrounding Cherry Creek Park, in addition to the numerous interior parking lots and access driveways.

The only existing through road in the park was a paved service driveway for the exclusive use of maintenance crews and police in patrol cars and other municipal employees. For everybody else the service road was closed during the day.

Throughout the entire year, from dusk to dawn, however, young couples in automobiles who sought privacy at night were permitted by long-established custom to enter the service road. They could then drive all the way to the duck pond and park their cars between the groundkeepers' workshop and the gardeners' greenhouse and remain there all night long at the water's edge until sunrise without being disturbed.

Nobody was certain how or when the custom of permitting couples in automobiles to use the service road after dark actually originated, but over the years the practice had been accepted by the police and the mayor's office and the people of Zephyrfield as though it had been so decreed and made lawful by the highest court.

Due to the nature of its use at night, the road to the duck pond was usually referred to as Lovers' Lane. In fact, a recently prepared city map listed Lovers' Lane in the index and identified its location in Cherry Creek Park.

("I can remember very well the first time I was taken by a boy to Cherry Creek Park and the terrible fuss my mother made about it when I told her where I'd been and that we'd parked in his car at the duck pond for about two hours that night. She was so upset and worried, because she was sure I'd let the boy get under my dress and do everything to me that he wanted to. I had an awful time trying to convince her that nothing much happened there that wouldn't have happened somewhere else, and that all we did was talk a lot and hold hands and listen to radio music and do a little hugging and kissing, and that was all.

("My mother had heard a lot of tales about what went on in Cherry Creek Park, and I'm sure much of it was true. Some of the girls my age and ones that I knew very well told me they'd gone there with boys for really making it and all that on the back seat of the car. After I went to Lovers' Lane that first time, and after that long lecture by my mother, I went back there with various boys many times, because it was so romantic and daring, and I thought making love there was the most delightful way it could be done. Naturally, I was careful not to say anything that would let my mother suspect what I was doing, and I'm sure she never had an inkling of my many adventures in Cherry Creek Park during the next several years.

("Well, now that I'm married and have two darling little daughters of my own, I often wonder what I'm going to say to them when they grow up. I suppose when that time comes I'm going to be just as upset and worried about my two teen-age daughters as my mother was about me.")

Soon after their marriage, Annette had been taken by Doan Thurmond to Cherry Creek Park several times to row around the duck pond or paddle in a canoe on the lily pond. Consequently, even though it was now very dark, Annette was so familiar with the wide tree-lined avenue leading from Eastern Boulevard to the park that she was quick to realize after they had finished eating and had left the Tic-Toc that Jack Summerall was driving to the park and not taking her to Evelyn.

Nothing had been said by either of them along the way, and by the time they had entered the driveway into the park and were within sight of the duck pond, Annette had already decided that it would be wise for her to try to remain as calm as possible, no matter what happened, and not say anything to displease Jack at a time like that.

Annette was well aware by then that Jack was confidently planning to use her as he wished, either with her consent or by force, before the night was over. Nevertheless, even though she realized how determined he could be to have his way, she still believed she would be able to prevent him from forcing her to submit to him by being as friendly and pleasant as possible while appealing to him to be faithful to Evelyn.

There were no other cars parked at the duck pond or lily pond when Annette and Jack came down the driveway, even though it was still only shortly after midnight; but almost immediately, as if it had been following them closely, an automobile came within sight and stopped a short distance away. The automobile had stopped so close to them that even in such a dim light it was easy to see that it was a city patrol car.

Jack immediately began complaining that the police had no right to follow him and charge him with a traffic violation when he was certain he had not driven through any stop signs or red lights and had been careful to stay under the speed limit all the way to Cherry Creek Park from Eastern Boulevard.

The policeman had left the patrol car, and waving the bright beam of his flashlight ahead of him, came up to the side of Jack's big sports car. He held the beam of light on Jack's face momentarily, and then, even more briefly, the light was directed at Annette before he switched it off.

With only a glimpse of his face, Annette was sure she recognized the handsome young man who earlier in the evening on Flower Street had warned her of being alone there at night and had advised her to phone somebody immediately for assistance. She wondered if he had recognized her, and if so, what he would think of her now, finding her in a car parked after midnight in Lovers' Lane.

It occurred to her that this was probably her only chance to ask for help, but she did not want to make trouble for Jack, and she was still confident that she could persuade him not to keep her there and force her to submit to him.

"Good evening," she heard Carl say.

"What do you want?" Jack asked in an unpleasant manner. "Driver's license? Car registration? What?"

"No, Mr. Summerall," Carl answered in a calm voice. "It's nothing like that."

Annette, opening her eyes then, could see Carl looking directly at her with a questioning smile.

"How do you know who I am?" said Jack in the same unpleasant tone of voice.

"Well, Mr. Summerall, in Zephyrfield we get to know

one another fairly easily—either by sight or reputation, if there's no other way. That's one of the advantages—or disadvantages—of living in a small suburb like Zephyrfield. And for one thing, I've often seen this racy-looking yellow sports car of yours wheeling around town, and I've always wondered if you have to make the ladies draw straws to decide which one you'll take for a ride. This is the first time, though, that I've seen your car out here at Cherry Creek Park at night."

"Okay! Okay!" Jack spoke out with an irritated sharpness. "So what's all this talking about? What are you after me for? I haven't done anything."

"It's like this, Mr. Summerall," Carl began, speaking patiently. "I happened to be cruising on Eastern Boulevard when I saw you pull away from the Tic-Toc and start driving out the avenue in this direction. I recognized your yellow sports car, and I was coming along behind you and admiring it when I observed that a caution blinker at an intersection was not working properly. I figured that you—you and the young lady—would be returning on the same route, and so I decided in the interest of safety that you should be advised in regard to the faulty operating condition of the blinker light so you'd want to drive cautiously when you leave here. The police department would much rather prevent an accident than have to investigate one, and so—"

"And so you followed me in a city police car all the way from the Tic-Toc to Cherry Creek Park and used up all that taxpayers' gasoline just to tell me that?"

"Well, the way it is, this happens to be in the area we normally patrol, and so—"

"So suppose I didn't plan to go back the same way I came? And maybe I'm not going back at all tonight. What do you think about that?"

"That's your privilege, Mr. Summerall," Carl told him. "And that settles the matter."

"Then you're not going to give me a ticket for a traffic violation?"

"Certainly not. But I will say that all this started because I was curious about the young lady with you and wanted to be sure—"

"Thanks a lot for being so goddamn curious about none of your business!" he told Carl in anger. "I didn't know my lady friend was attracting the attention of a cop!"

"For your information, Mr. Summerall, I was making myself available as a police officer in case—"

"And for your information, if I ever need a cop, I know how to call for one. And right now, I don't need you!"

Annette could see Carl watching her with an inquiring look while she hesitated to let him know in some way before it was too late that she did not feel completely safe.

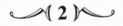

THERE was a sudden blare of static on the police radio-phone, and Carl went to the patrol car to answer the call. As soon as he had taken the message, he came back to speak to Jack Summerall.

"That was the sergeant sending me back to Eastern Boulevard to investigate a reported holdup," he explained. "But I didn't want to leave without letting you know that I've enjoyed talking to you, Mr. Summerall. Good-bye now."

"Don't let me keep you from your duty," Jack said with a swift wave of his hand. "And good-bye to you!"

Carl, leaning over in order to be able to see Annette's face more clearly, was again looking at her inquiringly.

"What makes you keep on hanging around here like this?" Jack demanded in his surly manner. "What the hell do you want now?"

Carl ignored Jack's questions as if he had not even heard them.

"Is there anything you'd like to tell me before I leave, Mrs. Thurmond?" Carl asked as he continued watching her closely. "If there's anything at all, I want to know about it, Mrs. Thurmond."

With her lips pressed tightly together as if to keep herself from saying anything, Annette shook her head decisively while being watched by both Carl and Jack.

After hesitating briefly, and without speaking again, Carl turned away and hurried to the patrol car.

"What the hell's been going on that I don't know about?" Jack was demanding angrily.

With tears of fright coming to her eyes, all she could do was hope Jack would not become so angry that he would hurt her in some way.

Nothing was said by either of them while they watched the patrol car go roaring up Lovers' Lane and pass quickly out of sight.

It seemed only seconds after Carl had left that the headlights of another automobile flashed through the darkness at the entrance to the park. After coming only a short distance down Lovers' Lane, and long before reaching the duck pond, the driver first turned off the headlights and then, evidently wanting to avoid being seen, parked his car behind a tall clump of shrubbery and switched off the engine. There was no sound to be heard from the parked car after that, not even the sound of a door being opened and closed.

As she sat motionlessly on the seat beside Jack with her fingers gripped tightly in the moist palms of her hands,

Annette was trying to remain as calm as possible. Now that Carl had left, she was beginning to regret that she had failed to let him know how uneasy she really was about being there alone with Jack Summerall.

Even though somebody else had come to the park and was nearby, the presence of another person there did not make her feel any less fearful, with Jack as angry as he was.

Just as she had been expecting, Jack suddenly turned to her with a loud outburst of anger.

"What a hell of a surprise you handed me! I never thought you'd be cozy with an ordinary cop! It sure made me feel like a goddamn fool when that goddamn cop comes along and knows who you are. 'Hello, there, Mrs. Thurmond! How are you tonight, Mrs. Thurmond?' Why didn't he call you 'Annette'? Maybe he was being nice and trying to cover up for you."

"I'm sorry, Jack," she said carefully, "but that policeman knew your name, too. He called you 'Mr. Summerall.' "

"So what? Everybody in town knows me. But how in hell did that cop get to know your name—'Mrs. Thurmond'! And while you're explaining that, tell me something else. Do you know what his name is?"

Annette nodded. "Yes."

"What is it?"

"Carl."

During the silence, which lasted a long time, Annette thought surely Jack was going to hit her at any moment.

"This is getting to be very interesting," he said presently. "So the cop's name is Carl, and he knows your name. I want to know more about your romance with a cop, but before that I want to hear about the doctor you mentioned earlier. You said you were in his house when you phoned for me to come get you. You said you didn't know his name, but what did this no-name doctor call you? Let me guess! 'Mrs. Thurmond'! Or was it 'Annette'? Anyhow, so you go around town at night telling strangers what your name is, huh? What a surprise party this has turned out to be!"

"Jack, it's nothing like the way you talk about it," Annette tried to tell him, "and if you'll let me explain—"

"I can figure out some things myself," he interrupted. "But right now I'm wondering why you acted so mysterious and wouldn't tell me why you left home tonight. What puzzles me is how you could fool me all this time by making me think you were such an oh-so-nice untouchable clean sweet wholesome ideal housewife married to Doan Thurmond and take-your-goddamn-hands-off-me-and-keep-them-to-yourself! It makes me feel ashamed of myself for letting you fool me the way you did while you were somewhere having one sex party after another. And when I brought you out here to Cherry Creek Park tonight from the Tic-Toc, you let me believe I'd have to spend a lot of time setting up a sexperience with you. How wrong I was! I bet you've been snickering at me for going through a lot of unnecessary motions to get you started when you've already had a couple of sexperiences so far tonight. Will you forgive me for being so goddamn dumb, Annette?"

"Jack," she pleaded, "if I could tell you, you wouldn't think that about me. If you knew how terrified I was when I was alone on the street and at that doctor's house . . ."

He put his arms around her and drew her so close she could feel his breath on her cheek. Even though her body was tense and rigid, she did not try to resist him immediately.

"Annette, let's not spoil things by having a big argument," Jack was whispering to her. "I'll take back all the mean things I said, because I'm sorry about it now. What I want to do now is tell you how much I like you and how wonderful I think you are. If you'll be a nice little sweetheart, you can have your choice of two places. We can stay here in the park and be romantic in a rowboat out there on the duck pond, or we can go back to Eastern Boulevard and get a room and have solid comfort on a bed in a motel. All you have to do is choose the place to suit yourself. It's lady's choice tonight."

As soon as Jack stopped whispering to Annette, he began hugging her so tightly that she was helpless to keep him from kissing her face and all over her neck. After a while, when he began stroking her body, she tried to struggle free, but had to give up when she realized she did not have the strength to resist him.

("I met Annette soon after she married Doan Thurmond and came to live in his big graystone house less than a block from where my husband and I live. Being such close neighbors, and having similar interest in clothes and cooking, Annette and I became very friendly and visited back and forth and often talked on the phone about various things. All of this was just a matter of friendship between Annette and me and did not involve our husbands, since they had practically no interests in common. Then, after getting to know Annette so well, it bothered me greatly when I realized one day what a terribly morbid attitude she had about Wayne Lombard, who had been her first husband and was killed during the robbery of his store.

("In her moments of frankness, when she seemed to have the need to confide in somebody who would be sympathetic, Annette would say so pathetically, with her eyes filled with tears, that Wayne had been the only love in her life and that even if she married a dozen times, all she lived for was to have three children she could raise in memory of him. I wouldn't think of mentioning this to Annette, because I'm sure she does not know about it, and it could be disastrous if added to her present state of mind. But my husband said he had heard confidentially that Doan could not father even one child for Annette after secretly having had a vasectomy operation before his marriage to her.

("Whether or not Annette ever gives birth to a child by Doan Thurmond or somebody else, that remains to be seen. But for the present the strange ceremony or ritual she performs like a memorial service for Wayne seems downright abnormal and morbid. I've watched her do this many times now. She will wash and dry and iron and then actually kiss every single button of a shirt that she said Wayne was wearing when he died. I've tried many times to suggest to Annette that she should do something to overcome her obsession about the past, but she remains unchanged in attitude. What I fear is that if this shirt-washing and button-kissing ceremony continues, and if she finds out about Doan's operation, it's very likely that she will do something rash and reckless, and I just don't know how a resulting disastrous event could be prevented.")

As he continued to hold Annette in a tight embrace, Jack kissed her cheek time after time and gently stroked her long brown hair.

"I don't know how I was able to wait this long for you," he whispered to Annette. "And now that I've got you at last, I don't intend ever to be without you again. You're so beautiful, Annette! So wonderful!"

"It's nice of you to say that, Jack, but it's very late, and so please take me to Evelyn now."

"But what about our sex party?"

"There won't be any."

"Then suppose I won't take you to see her?"

"Then I'll have to find some other way to get there."

"And what will you tell her?"

"I'll tell her that you brought me here and what you tried to make me do."

"Why? For God's sake, why?"

"You know why. Evelyn's my best friend, and I would never hide anything from her. My conscience wouldn't let me. In all fairness to her, Evelyn is entitled to know every word you said tonight and everything you did and tried to do."

"And you'll tell her all that?"

"Yes."

Annette thought he was going to strike her with his fist, and she tried to move as far away from him as she could.

"You bitch!" he said at once. "You and your goddamn conscience!"

Annette was cautiously moving away from him.

"If you said one little word like that to her, she'd divorce me so fast . . ." Jack was speaking rapidly. "Evelyn said one more time and one more woman and that would be the end of the line for me. And she means it. I'd get kicked out of the insurance agency she owns in her own name, and I wouldn't have a dime in the world after that, and nowhere to go. Now, would you still tell on me, Annette? You wouldn't do that, would you?"

"Yes, I'd have to, because my conscience—"

"To hell with you!" he told her angrily. "Go ahead and keep your goddamn conscience, and you'll find out how much good it'll do you. I'm leaving, and good-bye!"

"But what about me?" she asked anxiously. "Jack, what about me? I'd be terrified if you went away and left me here all by myself like this. You won't go off and leave me, will you, Jack?"

"You put me down good and hard after I brought you out here, and now all that begging is too late. You're on your own, and you can take care of yourself and your goddamn conscience from now on. I wouldn't stay around for a party with you now, even if you changed your mind and spread some of your sex all over the place."

Annette reached over and put her hand on his arm.

"Jack," she pleaded, "Jack, what would Evelyn think of you if she knew you brought me to Cherry Creek Park this late at night and then went away and left me all alone?"

"She's not going to do any thinking, because she's not going to know anything to think about. And the reason is that you're not going to tell her one single little goddamn word. Because it wouldn't be good for you—you might end up with a big ugly-looking scar somewhere on your face."

"Jack, you can't make me promise not to tell Evelyn," Annette spoke out defiantly.

"So maybe I can't make you promise. But I know how to make you feel sorry if you do tell her one little word, because for a long time to come you'll wish to God you hadn't."

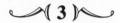

NOTHING had been said while Annette sat with her hands over her face and tried to hold back her sobs. Then, with a sudden movement, Jack got out and went to the other side of the big yellow sports car.

Without a word, he opened the door and motioned for Annette to step to the ground. When she remained where she was and made no move to obey him, Jack grasped her arm and roughly pulled her from the front seat of the automobile.

Annette was so surprised to be forced to leave the car that she still had not said anything when Jack reached for her small handbag and snatched it from her. After opening the purse, he reached into his pocket and took out a handful of coins and dropped the money into it.

"See what I did?" he said in a casual manner as he returned the handbag to her. A slight smile had come to his face. "I'm not leaving you stranded, am I? What I did was give you plenty of telephone money in dimes and quarters so you can get back into business again after I acted so stupid when I interrupted your nighttime profession by thinking you were just a nice simple little neighborhood girl who'd be thrilled from head to toe to have a date in Cherry Creek Park with me."

Jack paused for a moment while pointing at her handbag.

"Now you've got plenty of dimes and quarters in there so you can call up those cops and doctors and God-knows-who-else who'll remember your name so well. Mrs. Thurmond! Annette! Just tell them what your name is, and they'll come running. It's not like the old days, when a girl had to get out of the car and walk home if she wouldn't come across on the back seat. All you have to do now is drop a dime in the slot and ring up one of those guys."

Leaning against his yellow sports car, Jack watched her for a while before saying anything more.

"Any particular question you want answered before I leave?" he asked her then.

Annette had realized by that time that Jack fully intended, as a measure of punishment, actually to go away and leave her there, and she knew the only thing she could do for herself was to scream at the top of her voice. As she thought of doing that, she knew it was not likely that anybody could get there before Jack took her forcibly away to some other isolated place and left her in a similar terrifying predicament.

Even though her eyes were blurred, she could dimly see Jack watching her while he waited for her to say something in reply to his question, but all she could do was slowly shake her head. Her lips were pressed tightly together as she tried to keep from crying out in anguish.

"Well, I'll be going now," he told her with a wave of his

hand as he turned to open the door of his car. "I don't want to stay here and be in your way and keep you from getting back into circulation making house calls and such. You'll find several public phone booths up and down this driveway, and you've got plenty of dimes and quarters in your handbag. But if you don't want to bother about phoning now, just keep on walking to the end of the driveway and you'll be at the avenue, where a lot of cars go by all night long. Stand there and wave somebody down, and there's a good chance that either a doctor or a cop will stop for you and take you in. You know what to do then, don't you? Mrs. Thurmond!"

The powerful engine of Jack's sports car was started with a roar that echoed across the lily pond, and soon there was a loud screeching of the tires on the driveway pavement. Moments later the car's lights had completely vanished in the night.

Looking around her in the semidarkness of the park, Annette was surprised that she did not feel as frightened as she thought she would be. Just as it had been at the doctor's house, she had the feeling that it would be useless for her to struggle alone against what was bound to happen, and that only somebody like Randy or Carl would be able to help her. It was as if she could hear Wayne talking to her and saying there is nobody more helpless and forsaken than a young woman abandoned by fate and left to be at the mercy of the world.

Annette was still not worried, even though it was easy to imagine that there were men lurking behind the bushes and hedges and at any moment one of them would leap forward and strangle her or mercilessly harm her in some other way. As she stood there listening for the slightest sound, she was trying to decide whether to go down to the duck pond and hide in the greenhouse until daylight, or if it would be wiser to go up the driveway to the wide avenue and stop at the nearest dwelling and ask for help.

In a paralysis of indecision she closed her eyes. She seemed to hear a taunting voice laughing gleefully because she had been abandoned by fate and was helpless and forsaken. In a plaintive whisper Annette began pleading to be able to go back to her childhood and never have to grow older.

"If it had to be like this, I wish I had never grown up and could always sit on Daddy's lap while he smoothed my hair with his hands and called me his precious little girl and said he would always take care of me and never let me be harmed. I knew he loved me very much, because I could tell that by the way his voice sounded when he spoke my name. It was always so thrilling to hear him say, 'Annette, my precious little Annette.' I'd do anything if only I could sit on Daddy's lap now and hear him say my name. And then, when I went to bed, I'd have Mr. Truelove to cuddle with and keep me from being lonely while I was asleep."

Then something made her open her eyes. It was startling to see the figure of a man gradually emerging from the shadows only a short distance away.

At first she thought the man would fail to see her and go away without having known she was there, but he continued coming directly toward her. That was when she saw that he was wearing a shiny blue shirt that glowed even in the faint light of the night. She realized immediately that he was the same man she had seen twice before on Flower Street that night. It was odd that she had no fear of him now, and even felt safe and protected for the first time since Jack Summerall had gone away and left her in the park. After what had already happened tonight, it felt strange and unreal not to be frightened by the man in the blue shirt, not to want to scream and try to run for her life.

"I didn't expect to see you here," Annette said in a calm voice.

"Do you want to know why I'm here now?" he asked.

"Yes, I do. Why?"

"When you wouldn't get in my car the first time I saw you down there on Flower Street, that's when I decided to keep track of you. Then I followed you and that man out here to the park from the Tic-Toc and listened to you and him fuss and argue, and that's how I know what your name is. He called you 'Annette.' 'Mrs. Thurmond.' And I'll tell you my name. It's 'Willy John.' But I don't allow nobody to call me 'Billy John.' Remember that. It's 'Willy John.' Now, let's hear you say it right."

" 'Willy John . . .' "

"That's it. Now I'll tell you why I'm here like this. I make it my business to pick out women I want to keep from getting raped. Do you want to know how I got started making it my business to fix it so it wouldn't never happen to a woman?"

Annette was finally beginning to feel uneasy in the presence of the strange man, and she moved a few steps backward.

"Yes, I would like to know," she said, her voice becoming tense with her increasing uneasiness, "and then I'd like to go somewhere."

"Go where?"

"Back to where I used to be a tiny little girl and where my daddy was, and . . ."

"That sounds crazy enough to be what all that whispering was about awhile ago. I could hear it, but I couldn't make out what none of it was about. Come on, now, and let's walk down to the duck pond. There're some benches there, and you can sit down and not have to keep on standing up all the time."

After he had motioned to Annette several times and she still hesitated to go forward, Willy John grasped her arm and led her down the walkway. When they had reached the corner of the glass-enclosed greenhouse, straight ahead could be seen the sparkles of starlight on the duck pond.

"That sure is a pretty sight to look at, ain't it?" he said as he pointed at the sparkling water.

"Yes," Annette said at once, "and now I want to leave."

"You can't do that," Willy John told her in a forbidding manner, his high-pitched voice rising sharply as he spoke. "I haven't told you yet why I got started picking out certain women to keep them from getting raped. I had two sisters, and it worried me that they might get raped, and I decided to fix it so it couldn't never happen to them. Then, when I ran out of female kinfolks, I still had the feeling it was my duty to pick out some other women to keep from getting raped if they went out on the street after dark like you done tonight. There's only one way to put a stop to that and I picked you out to do it for."

"I really do want to leave now," Annette pleaded in a voice weak with anxiety. "Please, Willy John . . . will you drive me somewhere in your car . . . please?"

There was a high-back bench at the edge of the duck pond, and saying not a word in reply, he motioned for her to sit down on the bench. After that, and as her lips began trembling, she knew he was standing behind her to prevent her from being able to jump up and run away to hide from him in the darkness, because she could feel a hand on her shoulder. Presently he reached down with his other hand for some small pebbles and began tossing them one by one at the pond.

"That sure does make a pretty sight when the water ripples that way with the stars shining down on it," Willy John remarked in a pleasant manner in his high-pitched voice. "This is a good time to be here, because it wouldn't be pretty like it is if the rain was still coming down like it was when night was starting."

Willy John tossed the last pebble into the pond before speaking again.

"I like to watch those little waves start making a big circle and keep on spreading like they wish they could go around the whole world and never stop. If you never paid much attention to it before, now's your chance to get a good look at it while you can. You think it's real pretty, don't you?"

"Yes, yes, I do," Annette answered in haste. "But now I want to go . . . please. . . ."

"You stay right where you're at and lean your head back against the bench and look at the ripples on the pond and think how pretty it is to look at, and don't worry about nothing else."

With both of his hands suddenly tightening around her neck, and instantly frantic with fear, Annette tried to scream for help, but she was being choked so forcefully with the powerful strength of his hands that she was completely helpless and unable to make any sound at all. As she gradually became weaker and gave up struggling, there was a gleaming flash of starlight on the long blade of a knife, and then finally a splash as the knife sent waves rippling in endless circles over the whole wide expanse of the silent duck pond.